Long Beach
Short Stories

Long Beach Short Stories

Possibly Untrue Tales from the Pacific Northwest

James A. Tweedie

Dunecrest Press

Table of Contents

Foreword

The Long Beach Peninsula is geographically isolated and sparsely populated. Those who have lived here for any time at all know almost everyone along the narrow, thirty-mile stretch of beach. For a keen observer and good listener like Jim Tweedie, there is a story waiting behind each sand dune or whispered in the rustling of every tree.

"I just sit down and start writing," Jim told me once. "I stop when the story is finished." I don't confess to envy exactly, but for a non-fiction writer like myself, tied to endless hours of research and fact-checking, Jim's methods sounded magical. Later, when I read the book, I found his stories to be beguiling, enchanting and challenging in ways I did not expect.

As I read, of course, I thought I recognized a person here and there. Or maybe a circumstance sounded vaguely familiar. But just when I thought I had it nailed, along came that consummate storytelling twist—the *coup de grâce* that reminded me that it was just a story after all. Or . . . maybe not.

Sydney Stevens
Oysterville, 2016

Preface

Good stories entertain us, inspire us, and teach us something about ourselves and the world we call home. The world I am happy to call home is the historic and spectacular Long Beach Peninsula in Southwest Washington State. Fact and fiction mingle freely here, and a little bit of each has found its way into these Long Beach short stories.

I have made every effort to ensure that the historical information in this book is true, but I cannot vouch for the veracity of anything else you might come across as you stroll through the following pages. After all, fiction is fiction and possibly untrue even when it is true!

I am grateful to Sydney Stevens, Jerry Benning, Ken & Inez Greenfield, and Malcolm & Ardell McPhail for advising me on historical and factual details and to my wife, Jeanine, and daughters Ella, Emily and Eva, for providing insights and suggestions that helped turn good stories into even better ones.

If you are not already fortunate enough to be living on the Peninsula then reading these stories may be as close to the Beach as you are going to get—unless, of course, you are able to stop by for a visit! Until then, feel free to visit our Long Beach Peninsula web page www.funbeach.com and "read all about it!"

James Tweedie
Long Beach, Washington
2016

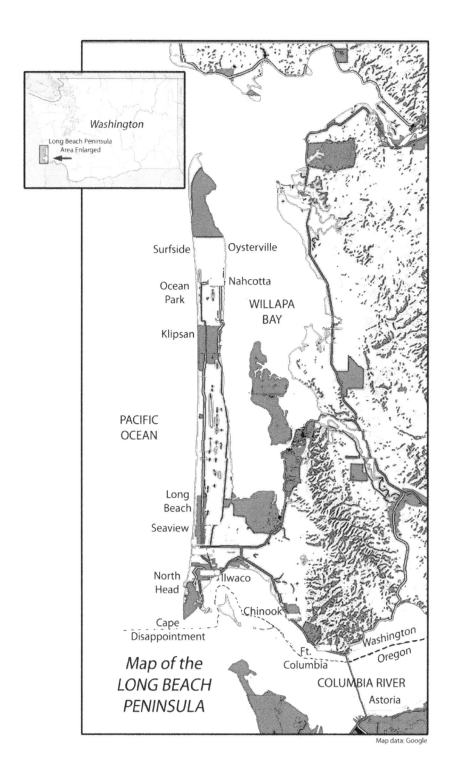

Map of the
LONG BEACH
PENINSULA

Sunset

It was only a ten-minute walk from Carter's house in Long Beach, Washington to the beach. But on this chilly, late-winter afternoon, the familiar stroll down the well-worn trail seemed to be taking forever. The usual bounce in his step was gone, replaced by slow and heavy plodding as if someone had slipped lead into the soles of his boots.

As he walked, Carter's stainless-steel clam gun dangled like dead weight in his left hand while his right hand found shelter in his front pants pocket; a warm and cozy place where his fingers mindlessly played with the shellfish license he had renewed two days earlier.

Clipped to his belt was a mesh bag just big enough to hold the fifteen razor clams he would be bringing home if he dug his limit.

With lips pressed tightly together and eyes staring unblinking at his feet, Carter pondered the fact that he was probably going to expire before his license did.

For two weeks, he had known he had cancer, but the test results the doctor had shared with him that morning had caught him completely by surprise. The doctor had chosen her words very carefully, doing her best to soften the news that soon, very soon, he was going to die and "there's nothing that you or anyone else can do about it."

Those weren't the exact words she used, of course, but that's what Carter heard her say.

Aside from some telltale jaundice, he still looked and felt as healthy as a 60-year old could ever hope to feel. But the doctor's words had changed everything. He had entered her office as an immortal. He had left it as a walking corpse.

A new script had been written for his life and now, as he wended his way down to the beach, he found he had already begun to slip into character and play the part. For the first time in his life, everywhere he looked, he saw death staring back at him.

Carter had been lost in thought, but the sound of the nearby surf and the approach of the final dune on the trail caused him to pause and look around. Stiff, brown, dune grass, stretched as far as he could see in all directions. Until this moment, the grass had seemed beautiful insofar as it gave texture, color and a sense of movement to the otherwise nondescript piles of sand it covered.

Today, however, the grass simply looked dead; a stark metaphor for himself as being someone whose own time had come . . . and now had gone.

Words memorized as a child in Sunday school flickered deep in the shadows of his memory: "All flesh is like grass, and its glory is like the flowers of the field; the grass withers and the flowers fade . . ."

To clear his head he took in a deep breath of the crisp, clean coastal air only to discover that today it seemed to carry a faint but undeniable scent of sadness. He did not appreciate the sensation.

As he crested the final dune, he saw the vast expanse of the Pacific Ocean stretched out and sandwiched between the "Longest Beach in the World" and the infinite sky. The sun, hovering just above the line of the horizon, was playing the role of Midas as it turned everything it touched into gold. Once again, however, the scene was lost on Carter. The horizon made him think of a "straight-line" heart monitor in a hospital room. Code Blue.

It was as if the poetry in Carter's heart had died and been replaced by prose written in the terse, cold style of an obituary.

He shook his head in an attempt to refocus his thoughts onto something more upbeat and positive.

I'm not dead yet, he reminded himself. *I'm not dead yet.*

As he walked onto the beach, he repeated the words over and over like a mantra, hoping that if he kept saying them, he might talk himself into actually believing them.

He found an empty stretch of sand and followed the lowering tide towards the setting sun, determined to invest all the life he had left into his quest for clams.

As usual, he enjoyed the hunt more than he did the clams but today, for some reason, the clams were showing themselves everywhere. In less than twenty minutes, he had dug up his limit. He had hoped it would have taken longer and been more of a challenge but now there was nothing left to do but walk back the way he had just come.

On top of the dune where the trail hit the beach there was a bench. Carter rarely sat on it but today, for some reason, he did.

Perhaps the clams seemed heavier than usual. More likely, the day itself had become too heavy for him to take another step.

He did not feel like going home.

He did not want the day to end but he did not want it to last forever, either. He felt ambivalent.

As he sat and watched the sun slip below the line of the ocean, part of him wished he could join it on its descent into oblivion. Part of him wished this but the rest of him wished for something else.

He found himself longing for something he could not find words to describe. It was not a longing for anything in particular. It was as though he was longing for a feeling. It was a longing he had known before but one that had been long forgotten; buried somewhere deep in the shadows of his soul.

Within moments, the longing overwhelmed him and he began to weep. He found himself yearning for, aching for a return to normalcy. Not the normalcy of life as it had been before today but a different sort of normalcy—a normalcy that was not simply the way things were, but the way they were supposed to be. Somewhere, deep in his soul, he caught a glimpse of a world made right; a world that, for the first time and at long last, was truly normal.

The feeling was tangible. Carter sensed this newborn world was close enough to touch—if only he could reach his hand out far enough.

When the tears stopped, Carter found himself filled with a sense of peace that was beyond his understanding.

He opened his eyes as the sunset reached its climax and what he saw was beautiful.

I'm not dead yet, he thought to himself.

He stood, took a long, deep breath, and turned towards home.

There were clams he needed to clean.

The Great Willapa Bay Oyster Rush

My friend David and I occasionally go off on what we call an "adventure." David is usually the one who comes up with a plan but this time I came up with the brilliant idea to go oystering. I'm sixty-five years old and the last time I picked an oyster was back in 1962 when I was eleven years old and my family was camping at Miracle Beach halfway up the east side of Vancouver Island. In other words, I'm no good at it and had absolutely no idea what I was getting myself into.

David grew up on the Long Beach Peninsula and knows just about everything there is to know about southwest Washington, the north Oregon coast and the lower Columbia—the river that keeps the two states at a respectful distance from each other. He does the oyster thing all the time so I was hoping that having him along might keep me from making a complete fool of myself.

If you want razor clams, you'll find them on the ocean side of the Peninsula. If you want oysters, you'll find them on the east side that looks out across Willapa Bay, one of the best kept secrets in America. If you don't live in the Pacific Northwest you've probably never heard of it. Even the tourists who drive along its shore heading north or south on US 101 aren't generally aware that it's the second largest bay on the West Coast between the Mexican border and Cape Flattery.

Before Lewis and Clark showed up in 1805, the Chinooks had the bay all to themselves. There were plenty of oysters to go around in those days. As outsiders began to settle the area, the tribe was generous enough to share them with their new neighbors. Soon a small settlement called Oysterville grew up alongside the bay where the oysters were plentiful.

Things went along nice and easy until the California Gold Rush came along. By the early 1850s, folks in San Francisco wanted oysters and were willing to pay up to a dollar to enjoy the decadent pleasure of eating one. It wasn't long before ships carrying oysters from Oysterville to San Francisco were doing their best to meet the demand. Within months, Oysterville became the second wealthiest community on the West Coast.

Years later, and for some reason no one has ever figured out, the native oysters fell into a decline. After an East coast oyster failed to thrive, a larger Japanese variety was introduced to the bay. The descendents of these oysters have kept the industry alive and well to this day. Oystering is such a big deal in Willapa Bay that local outfits have laid claim to just about any and every place that oysters will grow. Picking an oyster from one of these commercial oyster beds is tantamount to claim jumping.

Just south of Oysterville is a place called Nahcotta, and just south of Nahcotta's Port of Peninsula is a large, self-seeding oyster bed that is open to the public. If you have a Washington shellfish license, you can go out and get your daily limit of eighteen oysters as often as you want. The only rule is that you have to shuck them on the spot and leave the empty shells where you found them so new oysters will attach themselves to the shells and maintain the circle of oyster-life.

David and I pulled into Nahcotta during a negative low tide and started slopping our way through the shoreline mud with our buckets and shucking knives in hand. Finding the oysters didn't turn out to be as hard as I had thought. They were lying on top of the mud and all we needed to do was to bend over and pick them up. That was the easy part. Shucking them was the hard part.

The people who work for the local oyster companies and shuck oysters for a living can open up to twenty of them in one minute. In competition, the best of the best can shuck as many as thirty or forty oysters in the same amount of time.

It took me one or two minutes to shuck each of the oysters I picked up, which means I was physically forcing that small, dull shucking blade into the oysters and twisting them open for nearly an hour. That's hard work when you're not used to it. As a bonus, each time the two halves of the shell separated, oyster-smelling bay water ran out onto my shirt and pants. The mud on my tennis shoes added its own organic, seafloor odor and by the time we walked back to the parking lot I was glad we had come in David's truck and not my car.

The day turned out to be perfect except for two things:

1. I don't particularly like oysters; and

2. As a rule, Willapa Bay oysters don't have pearls in them, and even if you are lucky enough to find one, it will probably be small, misshapen and worth next to nothing.

That last point—the one about the pearls—was something I had known for a long time. David, of course, knew it, too, but on a whim before leaving my house, I grabbed a large, freshwater pearl I had purchased some years ago at a department store in the Philippines, and stuck it in my pocket. The pearl had little or no value but I thought it might be fun to drop it into David's oyster bucket to see what might happen.

When David let me off at my place, I told him he could keep my share of the oysters. I then headed into the garage where I took my shoes and clothes off because they were too filthy to wear into the house. Two days later, the garage smelled so bad I had to take the clothes and shoes into the back yard and power-wash them with a hose.

That same evening my phone rang. It was David saying he had found a pearl mixed in with his oysters and, after thinking it over for a day or two, felt morally obligated to thank me for the gift.

After we had enjoyed a good laugh, the conversation careened from one thing to another until we found ourselves discussing the California gold rush. The pearl I had planted in David's bucket triggered the memory of swindlers who would salt gold dust on an otherwise barren claim and fool an unsuspecting tenderfoot into buying rights to the land for more than it was worth.

I can't recall who came up with the idea but somehow we started talking about what would happen if news got out that valuable pearls had been found in the public-access Nachotta oyster bed.

Maybe, I mused, it would start a sort of 'pearl rush' or 'oyster rush' with people coming from as far away as Seattle and Portland to seek their fortune on the mudflats of Willapa Bay.

No, David mused back. It would never work. People weren't that gullible anymore. All they would have to do is look up "Willapa Bay pearl oysters" on the internet and see that there was nothing there.

But—I countered—what if they checked out the internet and found something that actually hinted there was something to the idea? What if someone planted a few pearls in a few oysters, planted a small, innocent April Fools story in the *Chinook Observer* along with a cryptic follow-up letter to the editor and, as the *pièce de résistance*, inserted a phony paragraph into the Wikipedia article on Willapa Bay. It might take weeks for someone to notice the internet ruse and edit it out.

One thing led to another and, after drinking too many cups of coffee, someone at the *Observer* wound up agreeing that it would be a good fun to put the joke into print. By the time the first of April came around the whole caboodle unfolded as quickly as the plot in a short story.

It turned out that David was wrong about the gullibility factor in the same way that Orson Welles was wrong about *War of the Worlds.*

Within a week, the number of people shucking oysters on the mudflats of Nahcotta had grown from the usual five or six people per day to ten or twelve. The following week the number had grown to twenty and by the last week of April there were so many people sloshing through the mud that fights started to break out over who had spotted a particularly promising oyster first.

Rumors began to slip and slide like oyster shooters.

It was reported that someone from Boise had found a pearl so large that they traded it for a four-bedroom condo in Sun Valley.

News reporters from Seattle and Portland picked up the story and it didn't take long before someone with a British accent was seen in Nahcotta talking into a television camera with the letters "BBC" stenciled on it.

By the first of May, the oyster bed had been trampled into oblivion and folks had begun foraging onto the private beds of local oyster companies. At that point, the Washington State Fish and Wildlife Department closed the area down and the

Pacific County Sheriff's department had to post an officer on-site to keep the wannabe pearl prospectors at bay.

By the second week of May, the hysteria had died down enough for reality to set in like a slap of ice-cold water and everybody breathed a sigh of relief when the hordes of fortune-seekers finally left the Peninsula. This included the local innkeepers who spent the next few weeks trying to get the stench of oysters and mudflat muck out of their guest room carpets.

David and I never denied the role we had played in the fiasco but we kept our profiles as low as possible until Memorial Day weekend arrived and "The World's Longest Yard Sale" changed the subject long enough for the whole thing to blow over.

As the summer months wound down the two of us met for lunch in the Shelburne Inn Pub and began talking about the upcoming razor clam season.

"You know," David said, "I've discovered a secret fragrance that brings the clams right up out of the sand. You spray the stuff on the beach and the clams try to jump into your bucket. They practically beg you to pick them up with your hands."

"Is that a fact?" I replied. "That's something I'd like to see."

"Hmmm," David mused, "I wonder if the *Chinook Observer* would be interested in running a story . . ."

Whistling in the Wind

"Daddy? What's that sound?"

I was eight years old when I asked my father that question. It was bedtime and my father was tucking me in for the night.

"What sound?" he replied. "I don't hear anything?"

"It sounds like a whistle," I explained. "Like two or three people whistling at the same time."

"I'm sorry, Princess," he said with a note of sadness in his voice, "my ears aren't what they used to be. It's probably just wind blowing through the trees."

"Are you sure?" I asked. "It doesn't sound like the wind, and it sounds far away, like over by the Big Road."

Back in those days, my family lived in Klipsan Beach, a small community on the Long Beach Peninsula just south of Ocean Park. As a little girl, I didn't know much about the history of the place. All I knew was that I lived with my parents on a small dirt road in a forest, and that when I took the bus to school in Ocean Park, the bus travelled along what I called the "Big Road." Now that I'm older, I know it is called the Pacific Highway, but even though it has a more

17

impressive name the road seems much smaller than it did when I was growing up.

Back then, everything seemed larger and grander, including the size of our house, the size of the Sitka Spruce trees that surrounded it, the size of the Ocean Park School, the size of Jack's Country Store and, as I already mentioned, the size of the "Big Road." The only thing bigger was my imagination—at least that is what my father liked to say.

"Use your imagination," he would answer whenever I asked him a question about, well, just about anything. "You tell *me*," he'd continue. "What do *you* think? How do *you* see it? Describe it to me."

"What's an 'imagination'?" I asked one night when I realized I had no idea what the word meant, or how I might have come into possession of whatever it was.

Dad thought for a long time before he answered the question.

"Imagination is a magical power everyone is born with," he explained, "It is the power you use to create new worlds inside you. . ." He paused again before adding, ". . . and it is the power you can use to change the world around you."

His answer puzzled me.

"I can change the world?" I asked. "How can I do that?"

"Well," he began, "let's say your mother asks you to do something you don't want to do. You know you *should* do it and you know you are going to *have* to do it, but you don't *want* to do it. At that moment the world seems like an unhappy place . . . dark and gloomy . . . and you might even think that your mother is being mean or unfair.

"But," he went on, "the world isn't really like that . . . at least it doesn't have to be that way unless you want it to be. What has happened is that you've used the power of your imagination to create that dark and gloomy world. That's the bad news. The good news is that you can use that same

18

imagination to change the world back into a bright and happy place. Take that chore for example. Instead of it being a bad thing, you can choose to turn it into a good thing. You can magically re-create it into a way to show your mother how much you love her, and maybe you can also use it as way to thank her for all the things she does for you each day. Is this making any sense?"

"Sort of," I said, not sure if I really had the power to do something like that.

"Sometimes," he added as a sort of afterthought, "the world really *is* a dark and gloomy place, filled with dark and gloomy people who really *are* mean and unfair. When this happens, your imagination isn't always strong enough to change it or to make all of it go away. But even then, your imagination will be strong enough to change the way you think or feel about it."

I can't really say that those were the actual words my father used. After all, I was only eight years old and this is not exactly the way most parents talk to eight year olds. Whatever words he used, Dad planted them like seeds in my heart, mind, and soul—seeds that continue to produce beautiful flowers and delicious fruit in my life to this day.

"You may not have complete control of the world outside you," Father told me that night, "but you can create as many worlds inside you as you'd like. Take that whistle sound you heard. I'd like you to tell me about it. Create a world where the sound can live. Use your imagination to give it life, and then surround it with a story. Can you tell me the story?"

Dad's question hung in the air like a piñata, daring me to take a bat and break it open to see what might be inside.

So, being an eight year old girl and not knowing any better, I used my imagination to tie on a blindfold, pick up a bat, spin around until I was dizzy, and take a mighty swing. I hit the piñata on my first try and what fell out was a story.

19

"Once upon a time," I began, "there was a girl named Flora. Flora was eight years old and lived in a house in the forest. When the sun shined in the sky, the forest was a friendly place where Flora skipped with the squirrels and flew high in the sky with the eagles. At night, or when the sun disappeared behind gray clouds on a rainy day, the forest became a dark and gloomy place, and no matter how hard she tried, Flora's imagination was not strong enough to stop the rain, make the clouds go away or turn the night into day. When the forest was dark, Flora stayed inside her house and read books or took out her crayons and drew pictures of sunshine.

"One dark and gloomy night, after her father tucked her in bed, kissed her goodnight and closed her door, Flora heard something that sounded like a whistle. It sounded nearby but also far away, both at the same time.

"At first she thought it might be an airplane whistling over her house, but there wasn't any place for planes to land nearby so it couldn't have been a plane . . ."

"Now Flora," Father interrupted, "it could have been an airplane. Didn't you know that years ago there was a small airport here in Klipsan? The Senior Center and Golden Sands are built on the north end of what used to be the runway . . ."

"Daddy," I said, "I'm the one with imagination and I'm telling the story, so even if there was a place for planes to land, the sound wasn't made by an airplane."

"All right, Honey. I'm sorry. Go ahead, I want to hear what happens."

I took a deep breath and tried to remember what I had been saying.

"Next," I continued, "the girl thought it might be a ship caught in a storm, starting to sink, whistling for help, hoping that someone on shore would come out and rescue them. But there wasn't a harbor nearby, and even if someone heard the whistle, no one on shore had a rescue boat, so it couldn't have been a ship . . ."

"Excuse me," my father interrupted again, "but did you know that a long time ago there was a life saving station in Klipsan? The station had special boats that could be pulled into the water and rowed out to rescue people from sinking ships. Later, the Coast guard took it over. The old buildings still exist and people can rent them . . . "

"Daddy!" I said as I sat up in my bed scowling. "*I'm* telling this story and even if there was a rescue station, it doesn't matter because the sound didn't come from a ship. I already told you that . . . Now where was I . . .?

"You heard a whistle," my father recalled, "and it didn't come from an airplane or a ship."

"That's right, now I remember. So next, the little girl thought the sound might be a train rushing past, whistling for people to get out of the way. But there wasn't a train nearby, either, so it couldn't have been a train . . ."

"Flora," my father said, "way back when there was a rescue station, there was also a train that went through Klipsan. It went all the way from the Columbia River and Ilwaco, up to Ocean Park and over to Nachotta. People called it the *Clamshell Railroad* . . ."

"DADDY! STOP IT!" I said loudly. "It's *my* story and I'll tell it any way I want . . ."

My father ignored me.

"Did you know," he continued, "that the Big Road was built on top of where the railroad tracks used to be?"

His comment stopped me dead in my own tracks.

"Daddy?" I asked in my softest, sweetest voice, "Did you say there used to be a railroad where the Big Road is now?"

"Yes."

"Did the train have a whistle?"

21

"Yes, I think so . . . no, I'm sure of it. I'm sure it had a whistle. A real train whistle, one that blew three or four loud notes at the same time so people could tell the train was coming."

"Daddy?"

"Yes, Honey?"

"Do you think that's what I heard?"

"What do you mean, 'Is that what you heard?'"

"I mean the whistle sound. Do you think it came from the *Clamshell Railroad*?"

"I can't say for sure one way or the other," my father carefully replied. "After all, I didn't hear it . . . but *you* did. What do you think? Use your imagination . . ."

I never finished telling my story that night and I didn't answer my father's question, either . . . at least not out loud using words. Instead, I remember smiling at him and saying, "Good night, Daddy."

He kissed me, tucked the blanket around my shoulders, turned off the light and closed the door to my room when he left.

As I lay there in the dark, I tried as hard as I could to hear the sound of the train whistle again, but all I heard was the soft, whispering sound of the wind blowing through the Sitka Spruce trees around our house. It was a beautiful, comforting sound, but even an eight year old girl could tell it was not the sound she had heard earlier. It was not the sound of a train whistle.

As I drifted into sleep, my imagination began to create new worlds to explore. Worlds where I flew up and over the Long Beach Peninsula in old airplanes with open cockpits. Worlds where I joined men who braved stormy seas and risked their lives to rescue passengers and crews from sinking ships; Worlds where I rode the *Clamshell Railroad* to Ilwaco and back again to my home in Klipsan.

I am older now and, if anything, my imagination is bigger than it was back then. I have learned there are times when I can change the world around me, and there are times when I can't. This has given me wisdom.

Yet I have found that in the darkest, gloomiest times in my life, my imagination has been strong enough to bring sunshine into my heart. I like to think that some of that sunshine has spread into the lives of my friends and family, including my eight year old daughter, Fiona.

When her father or I tuck her in bed each night we are not like most families who read their child a bedtime story before kissing them goodnight. We do read stories, of course, but the final story each evening belongs to Fiona.

"Tell us a story," we say. "Listen to your imagination and tell us what it says."

And she does.

Flutter

Most people familiar with Pacific Grove, California, are familiar with it for one of three reasons. 1. They know it as the site where thousands of Monarch Butterflies nest from October to February each year. 2. They know it as the location of Lover's Point, a minor Mecca for young couples who gather on summer evenings to pitch and woo, and take selfies with the sun setting in the Pacific Ocean behind them. 3. They know it as the Victorian-bedecked, upscale community lying between Monterey and the start of the famous "17 Mile Drive" that runs down the coast to Carmel.

What most people *don't* know about Pacific Grove is that it was originally founded in the 1870s as a Methodist church camp. The original name of the point was Lovers of Jesus Point, and folks from the camp would gather there at sunset for evening prayers. Instead of pitching and wooing, they would end the day by singing an appropriate hymn along the lines of, "Day is Dying in the West."

Along with individuals, organizations, state legislatures and both major political parties, Methodists helped lead the way during the American Temperance Movement. In part because of that influential heritage, it wasn't until the 1960s that Pacific Grove became the last incorporated community in California to legalize alcohol—thirty years after Prohibition had been repealed most everywhere else.

What—you ask—does any of this have to do with the Long Beach Peninsula? The question is a reasonable one, and since the teller of this story is a reasonable man, you can be assured that he has a reasonable answer to it.

The reasonable answer is that Ocean Park, now the economic and social hub of the north end of the Peninsula had its origin as a Methodist church camp. It was founded in the early 1880s just a few years after Pacific Grove. Among Ocean Park's historic buildings, the Lamberson cabin and Adelaide's Bookstore are among the few structures that still survive from that early, austere decade. The historic Ocean Park Methodist Church building, on the other hand, is a relative newcomer to the area, dating from 1914.

Today, a short drive on the main road north from downtown Ocean Park takes you to a sign that reads, "Ocean Park Retreat Center," subtitled, "United Methodist Camp." Here, the legacy of early Methodist community continues with church camp each summer, and secular as well as Christian groups using the facilities throughout the rest of the year.

So . . . after such a long and detailed introduction, what direction do you suppose this story is going to go?

If you are thinking it is going to segue into something that touches on religion, you would be wrong. If you are thinking the story will have something to do with abstaining or imbibing, you would be wrong again.

If, however, you are thinking that it might have something to do with butterflies, then congratulations!

Yes, you read correctly: Butterflies. Not the Monarch variety, but a smaller, distantly related species bearing the somewhat pretentious name, *Speyeria zerene hippolyta*, or, in more colloquial terms, the Oregon Silverspot butterfly. Until 1990, this butterfly was indigenous to the Long Beach Peninsula. Today, it is only found in four protected areas along the Oregon Coast. Depending on whose list you prefer, you can call it either "threatened" (U.S. Fish & Wildlife) or "endangered" (Washington Fish & Wildlife). Unfortunately, like a spoiled child, the Silverspot caterpillar is a finicky eater, one who is only willing to nibble on the leaves of a plant known as "the early blue violet."

On the Long Beach Peninsula, invasive species have pushed this plant so far off the map that the Silverspot butterfly can no longer find it. Folks from Washington Fish & Wildlife are working overtime to clear areas around Willapa Bay and replant the "early blues" in the hope that the Silverspots will pick up the scent and sign up for a repeat performance along the Washington coast.

In anticipation of its return, the State has set aside various tracts of ocean front dunes as "natural protected area and habitat for the Oregon Silverspotted Butterfly." Ironically, it is illegal for any unauthorized person to alter these areas in any way including, but not limited to, either removing invasive plants or reintroducing the "early blue violet" to its natural habitat. If someone is inclined to pursue either or both of these activities the best way to proceed is to pursue them in the privacy of his or her own "unprotected" backyard.

This then, leads us into the story of Thelma Mulroney.

Thelma Mulroney was someone who didn't care much about the subtle nuance of environmental law. She didn't care much about political correctness, either, which made it rather difficult for her friends to fit her into any of the current political or social shoeboxes that trend on Twitter. Thelma was someone who preferred to color her life outside the lines.

Take her favorite joke as an example.

A Washington State Fish & Game warden comes across a man sitting on the beach roasting a spit of meat over a fire.

"Watcha cookin'?" he asks.

"Seagull," the man replies.

"Why, you can't do that," the warden exclaims, "it's illegal to kill or eat seagulls."

"Oh," the man replies apologetically, "I didn't know that. I'm sorry, and I promise I'll never do it again."

"I'll let you off this time with a warning," the warden says, pausing for a moment before adding, "but you know, I've always wondered what seagull meat tastes like. If you don't mind my asking, what does seagull taste like?"

"Well," the man says after he rolls the question around in his mind for a moment or two, "I guess I'd describe it as sort of a cross between Bald Eagle and Spotted Owl . . ."

After hearing the joke, you might imagine that the walls of Thelma's house were festooned with stuffed birds and elk heads; and you might guess that her floors were covered with the hides of bears and wolves she had, with a smile on her lips and drool running down her chin, personally shot

You would have been wrong to think this.

Thelma, it turns out, would rather crash her car into a tree than run over a chipmunk, and the sudden splat of an insect on her car window was enough to bring tears of grief to her eyes.

Thelma was a complicated women and hard to pin down.

Take bears, for example. The Long Beach Peninsula has more bears per square mile than any other place in the State of Washington—wilderness areas included. At certain times of the year, the overpopulation forces many ursine critters to seek out extra calories by way of raiding garbage cans. This, of course, reshapes them into lazy bears who quickly learn that it is a lot easier to knock off a few trash bins than it is to dig up grubs or find berries out of season.

Thelma's solution to the problem of the bears was to say that folks should either trap them and ship them off to Mt. Baker or cull the herd and bring the bear census down to a size more in tune with what it would have been if there hadn't been so many humans messing with the eco-system.

As Thelma liked to say, "Sometimes you can have too much of a good thing."

Salmon were another topic of interest to Thelma.

"Take down the dams," she'd say at social gatherings, "and let the salmon be free in the way God intended them to free."

Her progressive friends would respond with smiles of approval—even the ones who weren't particularly comfortable with her use of the word, "God."

But, of course, as you might guess, Thelma wasn't finished.

With reference to the hoards of sea lions that gorge themselves on the helpless salmon as they back up at the fish ladder below The Dalles, she'd declare that, "The Fish & Wildlife folks should grind them up into fish food. Now wouldn't that be poetic justice?"

Her commercial and sports fishing friends would then pat her on the back, some of them convinced that this is exactly what God would do if He ever decided to reassert His sovereign providence over His good creation.

For some reason, rather than building enemies on all sides, Thelma's outspoken, independent, and occasional libertarian tendencies combined with her quirky but graceful nature to win friends and admirers in every circle in which she moved.

Part of this was because everyone knew Thelma was harmless. She had opinions, of course, but they never really led her to do anything with them. If actions speak louder than words, then Thelma's most outrageous declarations rarely amounted to anything more than whispering.

Butterflies changed all of that.

"Forty years ago," she randomly opined one evening following a particularly entertaining performance by the Peninsula Players at Ilwaco's River City Theater, "there were Silverspot Butterflies fluttering around my garden every summer. The undersides of their wings shimmered with what I imagined to be miniature, gleaming, uncirculated silver dollars. The effect was stunning."

Everyone within earshot nodded in agreement, even those who had never previously heard of the Oregon Silverspot Butterfly.

"I don't like the fact that they're gone," she said, "and I'm tired of the government taking so long to get them back onto the Peninsula where they belong."

For some reason, the little speech inspired her to actually try and do something about it.

The following March she set up a small greenhouse behind her Ocean Park home and began growing multiple pots of early blue violets.

Two months later, she headed south to collect Silverspot caterpillars from a nature preserve on the Oregon coast. It was illegal for her to do this, of course, but she figured that some of the butterflies probably missed her garden as much as she missed them.

I'm just bringing them home, she rationalized to herself.

In no time at all, the caterpillars were munching and chewing their way through the violets.

Towards the end of June, she watched as one of the caterpillars began spinning the first cocoon of the season. Soon there were cocoons suspended from almost every plant in her greenhouse.

In addition to the greenhouse, Thelma also invested a great deal of time and trouble in landscaping a suitable Silverspot butterfly habitat in her yard.

If butterflies have half the brain that I have, she mused, *they'll know they have a good thing and will stay put when I let them out.*

As the butterflies emerged from their chrysalises, her yard was ready and waiting for them.

For the first time in over forty years, Thelma watched as Silverspot butterflies fluttered about in her garden. To mark the occasion she purchased a picture of Kevin Costner on which he had written, alongside his autograph, the words, "If you build it, they will come."

It was all very gratifying.

It took Thelma a lot of commitment, a lot of energy, a lot of research, and a lot of years to establish a self-sustaining Silverspot community in her backyard; and she accomplished it without applying for grant funding, spending a single tax dollar, or having regulatory authorization to do any of it.

By the time five years had passed, laws had changed to where it was more legally acceptable for her to grow marijuana in her back yard than for her to attempt to reintroduce an endangered species into its natural habitat.

Word somehow got out about her little home garden project and late one summer afternoon there came a knock on her door.

"You can't do this," she was told.

"Why not?" she asked. "the butterflies seem to be happy."

"We're sorry," came the reply, "our hands are tied."

Thelma couldn't see what difference any of it made, but since it was illegal for her to be handling an endangered species without government approval her project was shut down quicker than the flutter of a butterfly wing.

As Charles Dickens' character Mr. Bumble once famously declared, "The law is a ass."

Sometimes, of course, the law is *not* an ass, but on the other hand, there are times when . . . well, you know.

Something to Sneeze At

This is a story about a sneeze. To understand the sneeze you need to know a few things about the person who sneezed it. His name is Gil Suomi.

Gil was born and bred in Ilwaco, Washington, a small fishing town at the mouth of the Columbia River. He had lived there long enough to remember the days when it had been the hub of business and commerce for the entire Long Beach Peninsula. The decline of the salmon industry, the growth of the communities of Long Beach and Ocean Park to the north and, most significant of all, the opening of the Megler Bridge across the Columbia River to Astoria, Oregon, had left the town no less quaint but far less prosperous than it had been back in the day.

Just up the river was the town of Chinook, where folks showed their good humor by wearing sweatshirts with the words, "Chinook—a Small Drinking Town with a Fishing Problem."

In contrast, Gil didn't have a fishing problem and he didn't drink alcohol. His father had done enough of both to convince him at an early age that he would be far better off finding vices of his own. To his surprise, he never found any that appealed to him.

Both then, and later, there was nothing particularly remarkable about Gil. It would be fair and accurate to simply describe him as a good kid who grew up to be a nice guy. He graduated from the local high school, married, apprenticed as a carpenter (where he acquired the nickname, "Punk"), and raised two daughters who grew up, married and moved away. He retired at 65 years of age and celebrated his 45th wedding anniversary two months before his wife passed away from breast cancer.

It had been a good life but his interest in enjoying more of it had died with his wife and been buried with her in the local cemetery.

After her death, Gil's friends and neighbors tried to get him back on his feet but after hearing him say, "No, thanks," to one invitation after another, they eventually gave it up and left him to himself.

After two years of eating frozen dinners and spending his waking hours staring numbly at the television, Gil woke one morning, stood up, stretched, took a deep breath, and sneezed.

It was not an ordinary sneeze.

To say it was loud would not have done it justice. It was a massive sneeze; a thunderous sneeze; a sneeze that shook the blinds in his bedroom window and sent his dog cowering behind the sofa.

Gil's eyes began to water and his nose began to run like a faucet.

He grabbed a tissue and crawled behind the sofa.

"Now, now, Sophie," he said softly. "It's all right. Poppy just had a sneeze."

As if on cue, his nose began to tingle.

He held his breath, but the tingle grew.

He held his nose, but the sneeze was not to be denied.

"AAA . . . CHOOOO!"

The blast knocked Gil over like an uprooted Sitka Spruce while Sophie ran to the front door, whining and whimpering as she desperately tried to scratch and claw herself as far away from him as possible.

Gil lay on the floor, listening to Sophie and feeling defeated.

"I'm all right!" he shouted across the room. "Poppy is all right!"

Some master you are, he thought to himself. You bring a dog home from the shelter and five days later, you're already scaring her to death.

Getting Sophie had been Gil's first attempt to start his life over again. He had never owned a dog before so every decision he had to make about dog food, collar, leash, and picking up poop with a plastic bag was a new and exciting adventure. As he had hoped, the house didn't seem quite so empty with Sophie in it and he had even found himself talking to her in the same way he used to talk to . . .

Gil let the thought pass and grabbed the arm of the sofa. As he pulled himself up, he noted that he needed another tissue.

"What's with the sneezing?" he asked.

He glanced around the room, wondering if his nose had finally succumbed to the two years of accumulated dust.

Gail would have never let things get this out of control, he thought.

He walked over to Sophie, picked her up and cradled her in his arms.

"Now, now, Sophie," he said soothingly. "I promise I won't scare you with a sneeze like that ever again."

Sophie did not look convinced, and Gil immediately regretted the promise when his nose began tingling again.

He set Sophie gently onto the floor and rushed through the front door onto the porch. He somehow managed to close the door behind him before cutting loose with another explosive sneeze.

The sneeze wasn't loud enough to stop a passing car but it was more than enough to stop Gil's neighbor, Potsy, who was walking along the sidewalk in front of Gil's house.

"*Terveys*, Punk," he yelled in bastardized Finnish.

"Stuff it, Pots," Gil yelled back, using the most refined English idiom he could come up with on the spur of the moment.

It was still early in the day but the mid-summer sun had been up long enough to warm the air and to cause Gil to squint against the glare. His nose was running again, and without a tissue, he did the next best thing as he leaned over the porch railing and drained himself into the long-neglected garden bed below.

Gil may have been a lousy housekeeper but he was an even worse gardener. Before her death, his wife had countered her husband's deficiencies with the touch of a white gloved finger on the furniture and the touch of a green thumb on the plants outside.

Gil looked around the yard and sighed. After two years without weeding or watering, the landscape was as dead and brown as a yard could possibly get in the naturally cool, moist Pacific Northwest.

Where there had once been flowers there were now . . .

Gil paused, marveling at the sight of a massive display of small, scrawny green shrubs with eye-blinding yellow flowers; plants that had sprouted up in seemingly random locations around the yard.

Cytisus scoparius, he muttered to himself using the only two botanical Latin words he knew—Scotch Broom.

The sight of it brought on another sneeze and then another.

He ran back into the house as fast as he could go and slammed the door shut behind him.

"Damn pollen!" he said loud enough to hear himself say it.

So it hadn't been the dust after all.

As his eyes readjusted to the interior darkness of the house, he remembered his father's long-ago warning to "keep away from those devil flowers. If you give 'em a chance, sooner or later they'll kill you for sure!"

Gil's father suffered from constant allergies his entire life and often declared that pollen would finish him off long before alcohol. Each day when he came home from work he'd pour his first shot of whiskey, hold it up, give Gil a wink and say, "It's allergy medicine, boy! Allergy medicine!"

What kind of medicine the second, third and fourth shots were he never bothered to explain.

Scotch Broom was not as widespread back then as it was now. Nowadays it's considered an invasive species, and attempts are made to eradicate it, especially in environmentally sensitive habitats. The seeds can lie in the soil for over 30 years before germinating, which explains why Gil's yard had become infested with the plant.

Ever since they inherited the house from Gil's parents, Gail had spent time each spring carefully pulling the new Scotch Broom shoots from around the house. Now, after being left untouched to grow for over two years, the unplucked sprouts had become large enough to bloom, spread seeds and guarantee their survival for another 30 years.

Gil did some quick calculations and figured that if he systematically pulled the plants out every year he would probably finish them off around the time he turned ninety-seven years old.

"Something to keep me busy," he said to Sophie.

He immediately began creating plans with both short-term and long-term goals. Like a contractor pouring over a blueprint he listed tools and materials he would need and what the final result was going to look like.

When he woke up the next morning, he was surprised to find that he was still sitting at the dining room table. His pencil had dropped to the floor and the paper he had been writing on had become spotted with drippings from his newly dysfunctional sinuses.

He stood up, stretched and started the day off with another sneeze. It was a good sneeze but not on par with the ones that had erupted from his head the day before. Even Sophie took the situation in stride and, perhaps out of sympathy, empathy, or a little bit of both, came through with a small but gratifying sneeze of her own.

"We're a team, aren't we, Sophie?" Gil announced as a smile began to spread across his face. "And like any team, we've got work to do!"

He poured some dry dog food into a bowl for Sophie, freshened her water, and grabbed a stale, half-eaten donut from a reused paper plate on the kitchen counter. While he ate the donut, he changed into his work clothes, scattering crumbs across his bedroom floor as he pulled on his pants.

"It's time for the knight in shining armor to slay the fierce dragon and rescue the fair maiden from her fate-worse-than-death," he proclaimed with an inflection worthy of Monty Python.

He clipped on Sophie's new leash and, side by side, they marched out to the garage. By the time Gil had grabbed a shovel, a pair of clippers and his old carpenter gloves, he was ready to engage the enemy *mano a mano* in a fight to the death.

His plans called for his first foray to be a sneak attack below the front porch and it wasn't long before he had silently pulled up most of the smaller shoots in the area by the roots. With the small fry out of the way, he lifted the shovel over his head, screamed like a banshee and attacked the largest plants in a furious, frontal assault.

It had been nearly two years since Gil had done heavy-lifting of any kind and digging up just one, deeply-rooted bush left him with barely enough energy to stagger back to the front steps.

So much for Plan A, he sighed. Good thing there's a Plan B.

As it turned out Gil had more plans than the alphabet had letters. He had prepared for every contingency with the same attention to detail that General Patton had shown during the Battle of the Bulge.

Plan B required him to pick up the phone and ask Potsy to come over and help.

Gil was surprised when Potsy said "Yes, I'll be right over." Ten minutes later, he was knocking on Gil's front door armed to the teeth with a chain saw.

After being convinced to trade it for a shovel, the two neighbors finished the area around the porch in no time, after which they pressed the attack to the side of the house moving in a clockwise direction. It was like old times for them both.

They enjoyed the day so much that by the time it was over Potsy had invited Gil over for dinner and Gil, without a moment of hesitation, said, "Yes."

It took the two of them three days to get the job done. When they finished, every joint, tendon, ligament and muscle in Gil's body was screaming with pain. The feeling thrilled him. He couldn't remember the last time he had felt so alive.

Through it all Sophie stood nearby, barking encouragement whenever she sensed Gil's enthusiasm was beginning to flag. Just like Gil had said, they had become a team.

Plan B had been a success. The Scotch Broom around his house was gone but the sneezing continued.

Plan C required recruiting his neighbors to rid the entire street of the stuff and Plan D involved petitioning the city council to declare Ilwaco a "Scotch Broom Free Zone".

By the end of the summer Gil had made enough progress on Plan C that he felt ready to put his name on the ballot for city council. He didn't win that year but the following year he was elected and the year after that—the very week he turned seventy years old—he successfully passed an ordinance requiring everyone in Ilwaco to remove Scotch Broom from their property or face a fine.

As it turned out Gil continued to sneeze every day and didn't stop until Sophie died ten years later. The coincidence did not surprise him because long before she died an allergist in Longview told Gil that the pollen in Scotch Broom was too heavy to be an allergen at all. What Gil was allergic to was dog hair.

Gil never mentioned the matter to Sophie but the choice he had to make had been easy. Until the day she died, Gil's every sneeze was a reminder of how important Sophie had become to him.

As for the Scotch Broom, Gil continued to hunt it down until he died at the age of ninety-seven.

As he grew older, Gil often told how his father had been wrong about many things but never so wrong as he had been about Scotch Broom.

"Dad called it a 'devil flower,'" he would say. "But instead of killing me, it gave me a reason to live."

And every time he told the story, he ended it with a sneeze, a wink, and a smile.

Blackberries

It was an unusually fine early September day in South-West Washington—a day with a clear sky, a warm sun and a cool Pacific Ocean breeze that chased the incoming tide over the Columbia River bar and up-stream towards Astoria.

"I'm bored, let's do something."

They were the first words Bob's wife had heard him speak all morning. Bob didn't say very much . . . at least not when he was at home. When Jean talked, however, words flowed as easy as water out of a garden hose.

"I'd be bored, too," she replied, "if I was sitting on the sofa wasting away a perfectly beautiful Saturday morning staring at the TV. Maybe you wouldn't be so bored if you took the time to turn it on."

She was right, of course, and Bob resented her saying it. He guessed that she would follow up her little jibe with a not-too-subtle reference to the "to-do" list she had handed him at breakfast . . . but he was wrong.

"Now that you mention it," she said, "I'm bored, too. I've got dinner started in the crock pot and we don't get days like this very often, especially on Saturdays. Forget the lawn. Let's go somewhere and do something."

"Like what?" Bob grunted, using as few words as possible.

"We could walk to the beach, or we could drive into town and do the Boardwalk . . ."

". . . and then," Bob interrupted, "we could stop at Scoopers and get some ice cream."

Bob didn't talk very much but when it came to food he could be quite chatty.

"You need the exercise," Jean replied. "You don't need the ice cream."

Bob's stomach proved her point. When he was fifty-five, his six-foot two-inch frame had been a relatively lean 195 pounds. Over the last nine years, however, he had somehow managed to add another forty pounds. It had all gone to his abdomen. If he still had a six-pack, it was going to take a disciplined diet or a plastic surgeon to uncover it.

"You're right," Bob countered after giving the matter some thought. "I don't need the ice cream. Maybe we could stop at the Cottage Bakery for a Devil Dog or a piece of pie, instead."

There was a short, awkward silence as Jean squeezed out a nearly inaudible sigh.

"I know what we can do," she continued. "Let's go to Fort Columbia. We haven't been there for a long time. We've got the State Park pass and it's a good place to take a walk on a nice day. As soon as I put on my shoes I'll be ready to go."

As usual, Bob didn't say anything. But he got up, put on his shoes and grabbed his hat and clip-on sunglasses. He was already in the car backing out of the garage by the time Jean came out of the house.

42

For some reason, Bob always found it easier to talk when he was in the car. It didn't matter whether he was driving or sitting in the passenger seat, he actually enjoyed the conversations he and Jean had when they were on the road. Today, the twenty-minute drive took them through Long Beach, past cranberry bogs, and then along open fields before turning south onto US 101 heading in the direction of the Megler Bridge and Astoria. Bob and Jean took turns talking and listening until, between the town of Chinook and the bridge, they came to a tunnel.

Although the highway now uses it, the tunnel was originally built to serve a small railroad that picked up ferry passengers from Astoria along the Washington State side of the lower end of the Columbia River and took them to Ilwaco, Long Beach, and beyond. The tunnel ran directly under Fort Columbia, a military post built in 1896 on top of a strategically located promontory. The U.S. Army built the fort along with state of the art artillery emplacements to protect American interests from any foreign power that tried to sail up the river with the intent of doing mischief in Portland. The army decommissioned the fort in 1947 and Washington State now preserves it as a historical site.

Just before the road entered the tunnel, Bob veered to the right and drove into the park. A left turn took him a short distance uphill to a parking lot next to the fort's old administration buildings. In recent years, budget cuts have kept the buildings closed except for summer weekends when volunteers are available to staff the interpretive center. Even so, the fort isn't quite the ghost town yet. Two of the upper houses are available for vacation rental, and one of the local repertory companies still uses the old theater.

None of this mattered to Bob or Jean. They had seen and heard it all before and in any case, the summer season was over and every building except for the toilets had been locked up tight. Without even glancing at the information signs, they walked back down the road towards the theater. When Jean noticed Bob was falling behind, she turned and watched him lean over the downhill edge of the road and stare at something.

"Watcha lookin' at?"

Bob reacted as if he had been caught with his hand in a cookie jar.

"Uh, nothin'," he said. "Nothin' much. Just some bushes."

Jean took a breath and started to ask why he thought staring at bushes by the side of the road was more interesting than walking next to her, but gave it up as Bob stuck his hands in his pockets and sauntered down to where she was standing. Jean then managed to shrug her shoulders, roll her eyes and take his hand in hers all at the same time.

Further along—down and around past the theater—a short detour off the main path led them to a rocky, sheltered cove on the river. On most days, they would have found a sunbather or two, or perhaps someone sitting in a beach chair quietly reading a book. Today, however, they had the place to themselves.

"Look," Jean said, pointing downriver where they could see Cape Disappointment in the distance. "Pelicans!"

Ten or fifteen pelicans were soaring and diving into the river where they had apparently found a school of small fish.

After watching for a while, Jean decided that when pelicans sit, they are handsome; when they fly, they are graceful; but when they dive, they are heavy and ungainly, hitting the water in the same way a watermelon might collide with a sidewalk.

After each splat, Jean watched as the fallen pelican exerted all of its considerable strength to get airborne again with wings beating the water until it achieved flight speed.

44

The scene reminded Jean of an intricately choreographed ballet.

The scene reminded Bob that he needed to call up his friend, Tom, and see if they could get in some late-season fishing.

Jean said, "Isn't it beautiful?"

Bob, of course, didn't say anything.

Instead, he took Jean by the hand and gave her a surprisingly tender kiss on the lips.

"What was that all about?" she blushed.

"Just seemed right, I guess," Bob answered with just the hint of a smile.

They turned and squeezed single file through the narrow path back to the main trail where they wordlessly joined hands once again and began walking back up the hill towards the car.

When they came to the place where Bob had paused earlier, Jean turned to see what had been so interesting as to stop him in his tracks.

What she saw was a massive copse of blackberry bushes rising up alongside the road and descending twenty or thirty feet down the steep slope below. The bushes were laden with ripe berries that seemed to be silently pleading with her to pick them, and render them into jam or bake them into pies.

This time it was Jean who stopped.

"Whatcha lookin' at?" Bob asked with an unmistakable twinkle in his eye.

"Nuthin'." Jean said.

"Nuthin' is what I have plenty of at the moment," Bob said as he pulled his left front pocket inside out as if to show Jean what "nuthin'" looked like.

For once, Jean was at a loss for words.

"There's some empty plastic bags in the trunk," Bob continued. "Why don't you get them while I pick a few berries. They'd be great with ice cream."

"No ice cream for you," Jean shot back, "but some berry cobbler might be nice. You go ahead and start picking. I'll be right back."

It took her sixty seconds to get to the car. She grabbed a few clear plastic produce bags, closed the trunk and headed back down the hill.

She noticed that Bob had disappeared.

Where the hell is he? she wondered.

The question was not rhetorical. She had no idea what had happened to him.

As it turned out, the mystery of Bob's disappearance was solved the moment she looked over the side of the road where the bushes were the thickest. What she saw was Bob, surrounded by thorny blackberry vines, lying on his back with his head pointed downhill.

"Oh, my," was the only thing she could think of to say.

In reply, Bob gave a little smile and then a little wave with his left hand. His right hand seemed to be busy with something else.

"Berries," he said after a few moments of awkward silence.

He held up his right hand and added, "and I'm not goin' to let go of any of 'em."

"Can you get up?" Jean asked, wondering if the preposition "out" might have been a better choice.

"Not without tearing the shirt off my back along with my skin."

Bob's smile grew a little bigger as he added, "I guess I'm stuck."

"Can't you just roll over?" Jean asked.

"And what good would that do?" Bob laughed. "I'd be face-down in the thorns and with no place to go but downhill. By the time I reached the bottom I'd look as if I'd gone through a paper shredder."

Jean stood motionless—silent and unsmiling.

"Just reach down, give me a hand and pull me up," Bob demanded with a touch of impatience in his voice.

Instead of sticking out her hand, Jean leaned over the edge of the road and said, "If butts were brains you'd be the smartest man in the world. You figure it out. I'm going back to the car and sit."

As she turned to leave, she could hear Bob shout back, "My butt isn't big, it's my stomach that's big!"

To which Jean replied, "Then that would make you the dumbest man in the world. Case closed."

The repartee made Bob smile all the more. As long as he didn't move the thorns didn't hurt much and, since struggling only made the situation worse, he decided to relax and let the scene play itself out. Jean, he knew, would eventually come back to get him out. The air was warm, the shade was cool and, as he popped one into his mouth, the berries were sweet.

Fifteen minutes later when Jean poked her head over the side of the road she found Bob still smiling but sound asleep.

"Wake up," she said.

Bob didn't stir.

"WAKE UP, YOU IDIOT!" she repeated as loudly as she could.

Bob stirred and after his head had cleared he announced, "So, the fair maiden returns to rescue her prince from the thorns of despair!"

"What?" Jean replied.

"Nuthin'," Bob said. "Just bend down and pull me out or call 911."

"I can't call 911," she mused, "the whole Peninsula would hear about it and I'd never live it down."

"Fair enough," Bob sighed. "Then that only leaves two options. You can either leave me here to die or you can reach down and pull me out."

Jean stood silently as she considered the alternatives. The first option was clearly untenable and second option was clearly impossible.

"Alright," she said after she had made up her mind, "I'll pull you out, but it's not going to be easy."

Jean got down on her knees and, when both of them stretched as far as they could reach, they were able to hook their fingertips together.

With a whisper that could have been heard a block away if there had been anyone around to hear it, Jean chanted, "One, two, three . . . pull!"

Their fingers came apart and Jean fell backwards onto the asphalt. She pulled herself up and looked back down into the bushes. Bob hadn't moved an inch.

"One more try," he said with his smile looking more and more like the Cheshire Cat in *Alice In Wonderland*. "Then, if that doesn't work, you can call 911."

"So be it. One more try," Jean repeated.

This time they stretched far enough to get a firm grip.

With the same loud whisper, Jean said, "Pull . . ."

She was planning to say, "Pull on the count of three," but as soon as Bob heard the word, "Pull," he pulled.

Jean lost her balance and fell in silence, landing on her back next to Bob with her head pointed downhill.

The silence lasted for a long time.

"I can't move," Jean said at last.

"Welcome to the club," Bob said.

"Now what?" she asked.

"Now you can call 911." Bob replied.

There was another long pause.

"The phone is in the car."

More silence.

As she turned her head to look at Bob, Jean felt her ear catch on a thorn.

"You know," Bob said. "I'm not bored anymore."

"Good for you," Jean said as she gently shook her ear free.

Although she couldn't see it, Bob's smile continued to grow.

"Any great ideas?" Jean asked.

"Only one," Bob replied.

"And what is that," Jean asked.

"Here," Bob said as he cautiously reached his hand over to Jean's mouth. "Have a blackberry."

Jean opened her mouth and corralled the proffered fruit with her lips.

"It tastes good," she said. "Thank you."

"You're welcome."

There was another long pause; a pause that lasted until Bob broke the silence.

"I love you," he said softly.

"I love you, too," Jean said.

And she smiled.

Second Thoughts

I never planned on robbing a bank. I mean, it wasn't on my bucket list or anything like that. It just sort of happened. Like when you're feeling depressed and you're driving down a two-lane highway late at night and you're tired and sleepy and you don't want to go home and you don't have anywhere else to go and you just want everything and everybody to just go away and leave you alone. Then you doze off for a moment and your head jerks up and you've drifted across the centerline. You catch yourself just before you careen off the shoulder and you can't remember how long you were blacked out but the adrenaline is pumping like crazy because you realize how close you came to getting yourself killed. Then you think, *My god, I could have taken out some poor family head on,* but you didn't and you're glad for that and feel lucky, somehow, that you're still alive.

Then the thought pops into your mind how easy it would be to drive off the road into a tree on purpose and then you wouldn't have to worry about going home or facing all the stress, the pressure and the problems that have been piling up one after another, like the credit card debt and being behind on the rent and the alimony payments and the girlfriend you

51

can't stand since she moved in with you and you can't get her to leave and she just sits in front of the TV and smokes dope all day, day after day and there's no end to it.

Wrapping yourself around a tree suddenly seems like a good idea and you're just about to turn the wheel when you have second thoughts and pull off into a turnout instead. After a twenty-minute nap, you feel refreshed and awake enough to drive home where you climb into bed and sleep until the whole thing starts over again the next morning.

Robbing the bank was sort of like that, except no one died or got hurt. I suppose the word I've been looking for is *impulsive*. I guess you could say that the whole thing was impulsive.

My name is Josh, and by now you've probably figured out I'm the guy with the dead credit card, the ex-wife and the stoner girlfriend. You probably think I'm a stupid moron or something but I have two graduate degrees and teach philosophy and comparative religion at a community college. I'm not dumb, I'm just apathetic. And if you're the one who happens to be stupid dumb then let me explain that *apathetic* is a word that means *I-just-simply-don't-care-about-anything-or-anybody-anymore.*

I used to care . . . really. I cared about a lot of things. I wanted to grow up and make something of myself. I loved reading and learning about different ways of thinking about the world, about life and what it all means. I liked puzzling over whether there was a god or not and, if there was, what he, she, or it would be like.

I had a philosophy professor who once asked an extra-credit question on one of his exams: "What do all the philosophies we studied this semester have in common?" When he handed out the grades the following week he explained that no one had gotten the extra credit. The answer he had been looking for turned out to be, "The thing they have in common is that they are all true." That's what he said, "They are all true."

I had no idea what he meant by it but I spent the next twenty years trying to figure it out. If I had been a pretentious, elite, academic snob, I would have been happy to let the undergraduates settle the question over late night cups of decorator coffees served by barista girls wearing scarves and peasant dresses in trendy, dimly lit, off-campus bistros.

Unfortunately, I wasn't pretentious enough to hand the question over to someone else. You see, the question actually meant something to me. After all, if every philosophy and religion were equally true then the word "true" would no longer mean anything since there would be nothing to contrast it with.

To concede such a thing might make life interesting but it would also make it meaningless. After all, if one thing is as good as another then it doesn't matter whether I take you out to dinner or hit you over the head with a brick. I mean, it might matter to you, but in the larger context of the universe, it wouldn't matter one way or the other. "Right" and "wrong" would just be two sides of the same coin.

In any case, I wound up reading everything I could find about the ways people think about "life, the world and everything" and eventually concluded that I had to either pick one way as being more true than the others or else succumb to the meaningless abyss of existential angst.

Lately, it seems to be fashionable among college kids to embrace what I call Spiritual Libertarianism. Searching for truth is sort of like shopping in the produce section at the grocery store. There are lots of fruits and vegetables to choose from and everyone is free to choose what seems best to them. In other words, what is true for you may not be true for me but as long as we don't judge each other and as long as we share a mutual respect and tolerance for each other, it doesn't really matter what anyone believes, as long as we are able to get along.

I can't buy into this particular worldview because it strikes me as logically inconsistent. After all, when the ideas of mutual respect and toleration are held up as mutually agreed upon truths, then anyone who says one truth is better than the rest is immediately condemned for being intolerant and disrespectful towards everyone else. At that point, and without being aware of the irony, you have come full circle back to the place where, in the name of toleration and respect, you have dissed someone else's truth as being less true than your own. In this case, it turns out that all truths are relative except for the ones you like best. I would rather wrap myself around a tree than wrap myself around a philosophy like that.

After twenty years of searching for an answer, I finally found one when my wife had an affair and moved out without even saying, "see you later." In response, I gave up on the idea of God, along with the idea of right and wrong, good and evil, true and false, good and bad, and all the rest of it. It turned out that my professor had gotten it backwards. The one thing every religion and philosophy has in common is that they're all a waste of time. After figuring this out, I chose Curtain #3 and won the Grand Prize: a meaningless life in a meaningless universe.

As best as I can figure, that's why I wound up robbing a bank—simply because it didn't matter whether I robbed it or I didn't.

The idea to rob it came to me from out of nowhere as I was driving past the bank on my way to the college this morning.

Why not? I asked myself. *And why not now?*

The moment hit me like *satori;* a moment of enlightenment so intense that even Zen *koans* began to make sense. I was surprised to discover I couldn't come up with a single, rational argument to counter the questions.

Without giving it a second thought, I parked the car, got out and, as I have done a hundred times before, walked into the bank.

"Good morning, Josh," Alice grinned as I walked up to her counter. "What'll it be today?"

I had expected an adrenalin rush but my heart was as calm and serene as the surface of a mountain lake on a windless morning. I felt more free and at peace than I had felt in a long time.

"I'll have all the money you have in your till," I said with a smile. "Oh, and Alice, would you please ask Phil to add all of his money to the bag, too?"

Alice looked at me as if she was waiting for me to say, "April Fool," or something.

It was getting awkward so I tried to help things along by saying, "It's okay. Don't worry. I don't have a gun or anything. Just give me the money. I have to get to school to teach a class and if you don't hurry it up I'm going to be late."

The awkwardness continued so I added the word, "Please."

Finally, I gave in to the cliché of replacing the smile with a glare along with the words, "I'm serious. Give me the money, now!"

To my relief, Alice pulled out a canvas bag and started scooping out the money from her till. She then walked over to Phil and, after whispering something in his ear, began to scoop the money from his till as well. I figured they were probably pushing an alarm button with their foot and dropping something in the bag that would explode red dye over everything in three minutes but just like everything else, it didn't matter to me one way or the other.

It occurred to me that I had elevated Apathy to the status of God and was laying down my life on an altar of self-sacrifice in praise and worship of Nothing In Particular.

Alice handed me the bag and I allowed my smile to reappear along with the words, "Thanks, Alice. Have a good day!"

No one tried to stop me as I walked back to my car. I tossed the bag in the back seat and pulled onto the street heading south towards the college.

I hadn't gone more than a quarter mile when I heard a loud "POP" followed by the sound of a police siren coming up from behind. Like a good citizen, I pulled to the curb as our small-town police chief zoomed past with lights flashing, probably expecting he would be chasing me at high-speed further down the road.

As I watched him disappear around a curve, my interest in teaching my morning class disappeared with him.

Why, I mused, *should I go out of my way to waste everyone's time by talking about something that doesn't matter to me anymore?*

So I ended up turning west on North Head Road instead of east on U.S. 101, and three miles later I parked the car next to the trail that leads down to the North Head lighthouse.

I grabbed the bag in the back seat and headed down the path, noting there was a red stain on the upholstery that was probably never going to come out. The peaceful euphoria I felt at the bank had already disappeared like the morning fog. Now I only felt tired. Sleepy tired.

". . . to sleep . . . perchance to dream . . ."[11]

A weary Hamlet spoke those words but ended up staying awake long enough to give someone with a sword a chance to

---

[1] Hamlet, Act 3, Scene 1

put him to sleep once and for all two acts later. As for me, I didn't think I was going to be able to keep my eyes open long enough to last until intermission.

I had reached the end of the trail. On my right stood the lighthouse and in front of me was a four-foot fence separating me from a 200-foot drop to the Pacific Ocean.

I swung the moneybag over my head and let it fly. I watched as it disappeared from view, unable to tell whether it had landed in the water or on the rocks below. I laughed out loud, struck by the absurdity of the thought. After all, what difference did it make where the money had landed? It was gone and that was all that mattered. And even that didn't matter. Not really.

"All hail to Thee, O Apathy!" I shouted into the face of the onshore breeze.

I hadn't planned on the couplet actually rhyming, but it did, and I laughed again, wondering if the world had gone mad . . . and if I was the only one who got the joke.

The words of my wise old friend King Solomon came to mind, words I could have written myself:

I applied my mind to study and to explore by wisdom all that is done under the heavens. What a heavy burden God has laid on us! I have seen all the things that are done under the sun; all of them are meaningless, a chasing after the wind.[21]

I climbed the fence and stood at the edge of the precipice, wondering if I would have any second thoughts, and, if I did, would they make any difference?

I leaned into the wind . . . closed my eyes . . .

---

[1] Ecclesiastes 1:13-14

"Excuse me . . ."

The words startled me. Without bothering to process a single thought, my socially-conditioned reflexes forced my eyes open and turned my head in the direction of the sound.

There was an older man with a large camera and an even larger smile standing on the safe side of the fence along with a woman I assumed was his wife. Next to her were four small children.

My inclination towards self-annihilation vanished in an instant— as if some transcendent power had highlighted the idea and deleted it with the push of a button. I found myself standing with my back to the ocean, wondering who I was and what I was doing there.

"Yes?" I said.

Why am I saying, "Yes?" to this man? Do I know him?

"I was wondering if you would take a picture of us?"

"Sure, I'd be glad to."

What am I saying? I don't care about these people. For all I care, they can go to hell . . .

"My wife and I are spending a few days with our family. They live in Long Beach and we're taking care of the grandkids this morning. I'm Bob and this is my wife, Harriet. We're from Boulder, Colorado."

"Hey, welcome to the beach. I'm Josh."

Why is he reaching his hand over the fence and why am I shaking it? Why am I smiling? I don't feel like smiling . . .

As I reached out my hand, I glanced at my watch.

"O, damn!" I said aloud, immediately regretting saying the word in front of the children. "I'm late for class!"

Suddenly it all came back to me: The divorce, the alimony, the debt, the girlfriend, the bank, the money . . . even Shakespeare and Solomon . . .

I spun back around, scanning the horizon and yearning for oblivion.

Meaningless . . . meaningless . . . a chasing after the wind.

Once again, I took a step toward eternity . . .

"Excuse me, Josh . . . about the picture?"

. . . and once again the smiling voice pulled me back from the edge.

The moment was surreal, absurd, irrational and ludicrous. I wanted to burst out laughing but found tears in my eyes instead.

For years, I've given my religion class students an assignment to watch the movies *Oh, God* and *Bruce Almighty.* Then they write three-page essays in which they take and defend a position on whether George Burns, Morgan Freeman or Jim Carrey come closest to the biblical idea of God. As I fell to my knees weeping in the shadow of the North Head Lighthouse, it occurred to me that I might have been wrong about the God thing all along. Instead of God being absurd or ha-ha funny, what if God turned out to be a God who smiles?

"You are God," I whispered as I stood and turned to face the man at the fence. "And since you asked, I'll take your picture."

I might have been out of my mind, but I wasn't crazy enough to think the old man with the camera was really God. But he might as well have been, at least for me at that particular moment.

I wasn't crazy enough to think I could get away with robbing a bank, either, but I was too busy taking a picture to worry about that for very long.

A new set of words from Solomon came to mind, words I had often read but never completely understood:

Remember your Creator in the days of your youth;
before the days of trouble come and the years

59

approach when you will say, "I find no pleasure in them." . . . *Remember him—before the silver cord is severed, or the golden bowl is broken, before the pitcher is shattered at the spring or the wheel broken at the well, and the dust returns to the ground it come from and the spirit returns to God who gave it. "Meaningless! Meaningless!" says the Teacher. "Everything is meaningless."*[31]

I had somehow misread my old friend. It seems he hadn't been saying, "Everything is meaningless" at all. Instead, it turns out he'd been saying, "Everything is meaningless if you leave God out of it."

Don't get me wrong, I'm not giving an altar call or anything, I'm just telling a story that happens to be about me. Things like love, joy, meaning, purpose and truth had been squeezed out of my life for so long I'd forgotten what they were like. But when God smiled on me with a wife and four grandchildren at his side, I began to remember.

I guess you could say I had second thoughts.

---

[1] Ecclesiastes 12:1, 6-8

60

You Never Know

"Yeah, I know what you mean," Phil mumbled as the conversation ricocheted onto the subject of bears.

There was a pause as the other three men sipped beer and waited for him to move the discussion forward. The Long Beach eatery where they had gathered for their weekly lunch echoed with the droning sounds of television sports programs and the chatter of departing customers accompanied by the clatter of dishes and table service being cleared away from nearby tables. The men were all in their seventies, and whatever hair they had left on their heads was gray.

"Well?" Rog poked after the pause became too long to ignore.

"Well, what?" Phil said as he took a sip of his whiskey neat.

"Well . . . what did you mean by saying that you know what we mean?" Shannon chimed in by way of explanation.

"I don't know what I meant," Phil said softly after taking another sip from his shot glass.

On a whim he had paid extra for Glenfiddich and was determined to savor every sip to the full.

Phil's companions understood this and waited patiently as he silently inventoried the ambient intimations of Highland peat bogs and heather in his beverage *du jour*.

It was 1:15 p.m. and in a short time, they would have the restaurant to themselves. None of them was in any hurry to go anywhere or do anything except sit, eat, drink and chew the fat with each other. It was mid-January. The weather was cold, there were no yards to mow, no gardens to tend and no "honey-do" errands to run. Retirement and the accumulated effects of age had slowed their lives considerably. If any of them had felt the need for a pocket calendar there would have been only one thing written in it for this particular day: "Lunch."

"Let's see, which of you ordered the mushroom burger and tots?"

Sarah, the server bringing the food was not the same one who had taken their orders.

"That would be me," said Rog.

"And the pot pie?"

Benny raised his hand, adding the words, "Guilty as charged"

After Sarah left to get the rest of their food, Phil continued.

"I guess it reminded me of the time I filled up the back of my pickup to haul some stuff to the dump. It was November 1st and the night before we had thrown a Halloween party for our kids and their friends so there were garbage bags filled with food scraps mixed in with the rest of the trash.

"Anyway, I went back into the house to get something and came out, climbed into the truck and turned onto Cranberry Road. I glanced in the mirror and couldn't see out my rear window. I figured the mirror had gotten out of alignment so I jiggled it around but it didn't seem to help. I turned my head to see what the problem was and noticed something large and dark blocking the window. It was the largest bear I'd ever seen. She must have smelled the garbage and climbed onto the truck when I went into the house.

"So? What happened?" Rog asked as he chewed on a tot.

"Well, she startled me so bad I almost drove off the road, but then I figured I had to get her off of the truck as quickly as possible so I slammed on the brakes to shake her up. She banged into the back of the cab but stayed where she was and I decided that having a 400 pound bear flying through my back window wasn't a good idea. So I floored the accelerator and tried to get her to fall off the back. That didn't work either. She seemed to like where she was. I wasn't sure what to do next. I didn't want to stop the truck where other people were standing around or in front of someone's house, and I didn't think it was a good idea to climb out of the truck with a hungry, seven-foot she-bear looming over my head."

"So? What did you do?" This time it was Benny who asked the question.

"I'd done some pheasant hunting the previous morning and my 12 gauge was still on the rack. I pulled off to the side of the road, slipped in a shell, checked to make sure there weren't any other cars in sight, rolled down the window and filled her backside with birdshot. I knew it wouldn't kill her or cause too much damage, but I hoped it would sting enough to change her mind about where she wanted to spend the rest of the morning."

Phil paused as the waiter returned with his French Dip and Shannon's corned beef sandwich.

"Well?" Rog asked as Phil started dipping.

"Well? What?" Phil mumbled with his mouth full of prime rib.

"What happened next?" Rog answered.

"That bear didn't flinch," Phil mumbled as he chewed. "She turned around slowly, as if curious to know what had

63

slapped her on the rear, caused the noise and filled the air with the smell of gunpowder. She stared right down the barrel of my gun, curled her lips back so I could enjoy the full sight of her teeth, uttered a low growl, and shook her head like dogs shake water off of their fur."

Phil took another bite of his French Dip and when he had finished chewing and swallowing, he continued.

"After that she relaxed her grin, gave me the saddest look I have ever seen and yawned."

"Yawned?" Rog interrupted, not convinced he had heard the word correctly.

"Yep," Phil said. "That's what she did—as clear as day. She yawned—as if the whole thing was boring and she'd had enough of it. She stood up, stretched to her full height, pivoted around, climbed off the truck and strolled down the road a ways before she made a right turn and disappeared into the trees. You never know with bears. I never saw her again. That was twenty years ago and I think there are more bears around now than there were then."

"That's true," Shannon asserted solemnly.

Shannon was the intellectual of the bunch, being the only one to have completed a graduate degree in anything—in his case, economics. He had come to Long Beach from Colorado where he worked as a CPA with an accounting firm. After he took early retirement, he and his wife purchased an RV and spent the next five years touring Mexico, Canada and the United States all the way to Alaska. They enjoyed the RV life so much they bought an RV park on the Long Beach Peninsula. After two years of catering to everyone else's good time it dawned on them that because of the business they were no longer able to enjoy the freedom of travel themselves so they sold out. Until Shannon's diabetes weakened him to the point where he had to use a walker, they had spent each winter in the Southwest. This year, however, they were staying home.

He continued.

"The other day I heard Thelma Mulroney cite a study that says there are more bears per square mile on the Peninsula than anywhere else in Washington . . ."

". . . and," Benny interrupted, "you think that if Thelma says it, it's true? What's she up to these days? Protecting our right to bear arms or fighting for stricter gun control laws? It doesn't matter what the cause is, she'll take one side or the other and be passionate about it until she comes up with something else to be passionate about. The woman's nuts."

"She might be nuts," Phil submitted, "but she's right about the bears. We've got lots more of them than we need."

"And people like that lady in Ilwaco don't help the situation, either," Rog added.

"Yeah," Phil said, "you mean the woman who keeps feeding the bears on her front porch even after she's been cited by the game wardens? If you ask me, she's the crazy one. Her neighbors can't even step outside of their homes without bumping into one of her pet bears."

"But what can we do about it?" said Benny.

"Maybe everyone should fill their garbage cans with strychnine." Rog suggested. "I bet that would give 'em a bigger slap on the butt than that old sow got from Phil's shotgun."

Roger Johnson was the newest member of the group. Other than that he had served in the army during Vietnam the men didn't know much about him except that he had recently moved to the Peninsula from California. When he retired, he and his wife decided to move to the Pacific Northwest. So they bought a house in Surfside and spent their days volunteering and taking walks on the beach. They had gotten to know

Benny and his new bride, Ruth, at church and it wasn't long before Rog had begun joining the other men for lunch.

Rog liked to get to the point as quickly as possible. He hadn't had much experience with bears and considered it easier to eliminate them as a nuisance than to tolerate them as part of the landscape.

"I've never worked with strychnine," Benny said, thoughtfully. "It would probably take quite a dose to do in a bear. And what they didn't eat would be picked up by a garbage truck, go the dump or a landfill and probably end up poisoning someone and contaminating the groundwater."

Ben Marshall was an entrepreneur, especially when it came to investing in property. "Land rich and cash poor," was the cliché he used to describe himself. His interest in land acquisition had required him to become somewhat of an expert on the subject of environmental laws—most of which he ardently supported. He was a lifetime member of Ducks Unlimited and over the years had actually donated hundreds of acres of undeveloped wetlands to the organization.

"No," he continued, "if you want to be free of bears there's only one way to go about it."

The table became silent as each man leaned forward to hear Benny's solution to the bear problem.

"All you have to do, "he said, ". . . is move to Hawaii."

When the groans died down Benny chipped in another thought.

"It reminds me of the hymn we used to sing at church when I was growing up. At the time I thought we were singing about a grizzly with eye problems."

"And . . ." Shannon asked, taking the bait, " . . . that hymn would be . . .?"

"'Gladly, the Cross I'd Bear,' of course," Rog answered.

"I'm sorry I asked," Shannon sighed.

"Speaking of bears," Rog continued, "I knew a man in Colorado who was an expert on Grizzlies. He researched them, tracked them in the wilds and knew more about them than just about anyone. He knew better than most people how dangerous they can be so he always kept his distance and only observed them with binoculars. One day he was up in Glacier National Park hiking in the back country when he came around a corner and startled a Grizzly who had found a bush full of ripe berries. Before he could back away, the bear took a swipe at him with his paw and tore one side of his face clean off. It was a miracle he survived."

"You never know with bears," Phil said, nodding his head in agreement with himself.

"Yep," Shannon echoed, "you never know. The funny thing is the guy didn't blame the bear. The way he saw it, the bear was just being a bear and he was the one who messed up. After a bunch of plastic surgeries, he headed straight back to researching Grizzlies in the wild."

Phil continued nodding his head as he added, "There's a lot of those big bears in Glacier and Yellowstone. Years ago, not long after we were first married, Char and I went camping up into Banff and Jasper. On the way, we stopped at the Many Glacier Lodge at Swiftcurrent Lake in Glacier. We went to take a short walk over to Josephine Lake for a better view of Mt. Grinnell but the trail was closed off with yellow tape and a warning sign. The sign said that a Grizzly had been observed, "exhibiting unusual behavior." When we got back to the lodge, we asked a ranger what the "unusual behavior" was all about. He told us there was a large snow bank on the far side of Josephine Lake and a bear had been seen climbing up the slope onto the snow, flopping on its back, and sliding down the snow bank with its paws waving in the air. According to the ranger, the bear did this repeatedly and appeared to be enjoying himself immensely. Like I already said, 'You never know.'"

Phil had grown up on the Peninsula and graduated from Ilwaco High School. He'd sold insurance for a living and had enjoyed camping, hunting, fishing and just about anything else that could be done outdoors. Arthritis had taken its toll, however, and he used a cane to ease the pain. The way he saw it, taking a shot of whiskey every so often didn't hurt, either.

Benny glanced at his watch

"It's 2:30 already," he said. "I've gotta go. I promised Ruth I'd be home in time to meet with the plumber. He said he'd be at the house between 3:00 and 5:00 p.m. but, like Phil says, you never know.

The men surveyed their empty plates and empty glasses.

"This was good," Shannon spoke. "Next week; same time, same place? Okay?"

Each man nodded his head and offered a soft grunt of affirmation. Phil grabbed his cane and Shannon grabbed his walker as the four of them slowly made their way to the cash register to pay for the lunch.

A nervous-looking man who, from the back at least, appeared to be in his early 20s was ahead of them and Sarah, the only server left in the room was standing as still as death behind the open till.

As they came up from behind, the man turned and brandished an unsheathed hunting knife in the air. His head and face were covered by a black balaclava.

"Come on, you old farts. You've already got your wallets out so just put them on the counter next to the till and no one will get hurt, okay? Just hurry up. Do it, now!"

With a nervous glance at one another Phil, Shannon and Benny complied, but Rog paused just long enough to test the man's patience.

"Hand it over, Pops!" he demanded as he waved the knife in Rog's direction.

Rog responded by letting his wallet drop to the floor while simultaneously bringing his right leg up in a blur. His foot hit the man's wrist and sent the knife flying into the air where it buried itself point first into the ceiling. With breathtaking speed, Rog regained his stance, lunged forwards, grabbed the man by the front of his shirt, twisted him down to the ground like a sack of wheat and planted a foot on his throat. The whole thing took less than two seconds.

"Call 911, Sarah," Rog said calmly.

"And as for you," he added glaring down at the man on the floor. "If you so much as twitch I will kick you in the groin so hard you'll be singing soprano in the prison choir for the rest of your life."

The man did not twitch.

An hour later, after the Long Beach police and other law enforcement officers had left the scene and after phone calls had been made to tell their wives they would be getting home later than planned, the four men were back at the same table drinking coffee served "on the house" by Sarah.

It was Shannon who finally came out with the obvious question.

"Where in Sam Hill did you learn to do that?" he asked.

Rog stared at his coffee for a long time before he gave an answer.

"Special Forces," he said. "Green Berets."

He took another sip of coffee before adding, "And then, after I got out of the army, I taught martial arts for fifteen years."

Rog lifted his head and looked at his three friends with a smile.

"My civilian *Sensei* taught that we should always think of Judo or Karate as arts of self-defense. Even when we attack, the first priority is always to protect ourselves. Sensei used to say the best form of self-defense is to walk or run away from a potential situation—especially if a gun or a knife is involved."

"So, why did you attack this guy?" Benny asked.

"He seemed to be high on something, or psychotic. He was acting irrationally and recklessly. He was a clear danger to all of us. Even so, I would have let him get away with it except for two things."

"And those two things were?"

This time the question came from Phil.

"Well first of all, he was holding the knife like it was an ice cream cone. It would have been almost impossible for it to have gotten in the way of my foot."

"And the second thing?" Phil asked again.

"When he looked at us he saw four old men who posed no threat to him at all. He wrote us off as weak and feeble and so he let his guard down. This gave me the edge I needed. He had no idea what hit him."

"Neither did we," said Shannon.

"You never know," said Phil.

The Ransom of Blue Chief

Thomas Theophilos Tuppencethaler was seven years old and liked almost everything in the world—except for his parents, his five year-old sister, his older brother, and his name. He didn't mind being called Tommy, but his other names were too long and complicated for a boy of his age and sensibility.

If you asked him why he didn't like his parents, he would say that it was because they were always telling him what to do.

For example, in the middle of an otherwise pleasant dinner, they would spoil the whole thing by saying something like, "Eat your peas. No computer games for you unless you eat every one of your peas," or, after dinner, they would say things like, "Tommy, stop teasing the cat."

When they weren't telling him what to do they were poking their noses into his personal affairs by asking questions like, "Did you finish your homework?" or "Tommy, did you grind Silly Putty into the carpet again?"

Tommy didn't want his parents to go away, or anything like that, he just wanted them to leave him alone and treat him more like an adult—like they did Steve.

Steve was sixteen. Before Tommy was born, when his mother married Tommy's father, his father already had Steve from his first marriage. That was why Steve was so much older than Tommy. Tommy didn't like Steve because he got to do things like drive a car, go to high school, date girls, play the saxophone and go to church youth group on Friday evenings.

Tommy wasn't interested in dating girls but the rest of it seemed unfair. Their church didn't have a youth group for seven year-olds. He had to put up with one teacher at school all day while Steve had five or six different classes with a different teacher in each one. He had to take piano lessons (which were boring). And he had to walk or get a ride from someone to get anywhere.

He also didn't like Steve because Steve was never around to play with or talk to or things like that. Whenever he was home, Steve spent his time texting on his phone and listening to music through his ear buds. Tommy wasn't sure Steve even knew he existed.

And then there was Tara. It wasn't her fault Tommy didn't like her. She was about as nice as a little sister could be and she was someone to play with when Tommy didn't have anything better to do.

Even so, Tommy didn't like her because she got to wear new clothes while he had to wear Steve's hand-me-downs his parents kept in an old cardboard box in the garage. He didn't like Tara because everyone said she was "cute" and nobody ever said that he was cute anymore.

He never heard his parents yell at Tara but it seemed as if they were always yelling at him. With Tara, his parents would say things like, "Good job, Tara." With him they would say things like, "That was not a nice thing to say to Mrs. Monroe, was it, Tommy?"

On the plus side, the one thing Tommy liked more than anything else was blueberries.

For breakfast, Tommy liked them on his cold cereal, in his oatmeal, and mixed into his pancakes. He didn't particularly like salads, but if they had blueberries in them he would at least eat the blueberries. For a snack, he liked blueberry muffins and for dessert, he liked blueberry cobbler with vanilla ice cream.

The blueberries that Tommy liked best were the ones he and his family picked each summer at the blueberry farm on Sandridge Road. His parents said that blueberries grew on bushes but to Tommy the bushes seemed more like trees. Even his father wasn't tall enough to reach the highest berries without a ladder.

If he had lived close enough to the farm to walk to it, Tommy would have spent every day picking and eating blueberries. Unfortunately, because his house was at the far north end of the Long Beach Peninsula in Surfside, and the blueberry farm was at the southern end of the Peninsula near Long Beach, he could only go when his parents took him there on a family outing.

One Saturday morning in August when Tommy heard his father say, "Who wants to pick blueberries?" Tommy was the first one in the house to say, "*I'll* go!"

As it turned out all five Tuppencethalers went to the blueberry farm that day.

After Tommy's father parked the car alongside the gravel road that ran through the farm they walked into a wooden shed where the farm owners kept empty cans and cardboard boxes to hold the blueberries. Next to the boxes was a weighing scale and a sign that said how much to pay for every pound of blueberries. There was also a small wooden box bolted to the old wooden counter with a padlock on the side and a slot in the top where people could put their money.

Since the farm stretched out over several acres Tommy's father reminded everyone to keep within shouting distance of each other. Before they started picking, however, Tommy's mother took him aside and said, "Now don't get blueberry juice all over your clothes like you did last time. What a mess!"

Tommy couldn't see why she made such a big deal about it because, just like today, he had only been wearing some of Steve's old clothes—clothes that Tommy thought should have been thrown out when Steve had outgrown them nine years earlier.

After all the speeches were over, Tara wandered off with her mother, Steve sat on the ground listening to music—idly picking berries from the lowest branches of the bush closest to the car—and Tommy's father began stretching as high up as he could to get the larger berries that other people hadn't been able to reach.

As usual, nobody was paying any attention to Tommy, so he headed off to a special place where he knew the bushes had the sweetest berries. There were always plenty of blueberries there because the bushes were so overgrown with blackberry vines that only someone seven years-old or smaller could have crawled inside.

After squirming his way in for twenty feet or so, there was an open space where Tommy could stand up. It felt like a fort to Tommy. It was a place where he felt grown up and independent. It was a place where nobody told him what to do and where nobody yelled at him. It was quiet, it was shady, and he didn't have to share it with anybody. Best of all, there were ripe blueberries and blackberries everywhere.

When he picked blueberries, Tommy had a system. After dropping ten berries into his can, he always ate the next one he picked. This usually meant that when his father called for everybody to meet back at the car after an hour or so,

Tommy's can had fewer berries in it than anyone else's. On the other hand, because Tommy's stomach had more berries in it than anyone else's he figured it all sort-of came out even

People at his church were always talking about Heaven, but if Heaven was all clouds and angels then Tommy couldn't understand why everyone made such a fuss about it. As far as he was concerned, if Heaven didn't have blueberries then he wasn't particularly interested in going there, especially if it was "for ever and ever . . . world without end. Amen."

For Tommy, the closest thing to Heaven he could imagine was where he was right then, safe and cozy in his secret fort. As far as he could tell, nobody knew where he was, and that was just fine with him.

After a short while, the morning clouds disappeared and the sun began spreading light and warmth on everything it touched. Tommy could hear bees buzzing in the bushes and could see ants crawling on branches looking for something sweet to take back to their nests. He could hear birds chirping and sometimes he could see them silhouetted against the sky as they hopped through the blueberry leaves above his head.

As he picked and ate his blueberries Tommy recalled what his mother had said about not getting blueberry juice on his clothes. After remembering what she had said, he started thinking about it and the more he thought about it the less he liked thinking about it.

Just for once, he said to himself, *I'm going to do what I want to do.*

Thinking this thought made him feel more grown up than he felt before he thought of it. But thinking the thought also forced him to face up to a very important question: What exactly *did* he want to do?

After pondering the matter for a few moments, he came to a surprising conclusion:

I want to be an Indian, he announced silently to himself.

To make it official, he took a handful of blueberries, squished them in his hands, and drew blue war paint all over his face. When he was done, he tried licking the leftover juice off his hands, but because they still looked wet and felt sticky, he gave it up and wiped them on the front of his t-shirt, instead.

All of this made Tommy feel more and more free and independent.

I could stay here forever, he thought to himself. *I like it here. Why should I even bother to go home?*

In the distance, he heard his father's voice. His father seemed to be shouting, but although Tommy was too far away to hear what he was saying, he knew what the shouting meant. It meant that it was time for everyone to meet back at the car. Tommy figured his father was shouting because he couldn't find Tommy and had no idea where he was.

When this happened before, Tommy always scurried out from wherever he was hiding and ran as fast as he could to the car. He did this for two reasons: The first reason was that he didn't want to be yelled at or get in trouble for making everyone wait, and the second reason was that he was afraid his parents would drive home without him.

Today, however, none of this worried him enough to cause him to abandon his fort. Instead, he found himself thinking thoughts he had never thought before.

Everyone is always telling me what to do, he reasoned. *If it's ever going to stop it might as well be right now.*

He felt defiant, brave and grown up—not in an adult way, but in a Peter Pan sort of way in which he was able to live in both the world of childhood and the world of complete and total freedom at the same time. He felt so excited about this that he stood up, beat his chest and crowed, just like he had seen Peter Pan do in the Disney movie. Tommy knew that in Peter's Never-Land, the Indians had been Peter's rivals, but in

76

Tommy's Never-Land, he saw no reason why he couldn't be both at the same time.

He suddenly pictured his father as Captain Hook, and that image made him even more determined to hold his ground, even if it meant a fight to the death!

To his surprise, he found the thought of his parents driving away without him no longer frightened him. He even began to hope it would happen. As soon as they were gone, he would crawl out of his fort and have the entire blueberry farm to himself.

Back at the car, Tommy's father was starting to lose his patience.

"That Tommy needs a good talking to," he grumbled. "If he doesn't show up here in the next five minutes he's going to be grounded for the rest of the summer."

"C'mon, Dad," Steve interrupted. "Cut him some slack. He's just a kid. He's probably wandered off somewhere and doesn't know what time it is."

"That's no excuse," his father answered. "He shouldn't have wandered off in the ..."

"Dear," Tommy's mother interrupted in a soft and calming tone, "let's just slow down, okay? We don't know why he's not here. We can decide what to do after we find him Let's split up and look for him and then, in fifteen minutes, meet somewhere along the ditch that divides the farm in half. Tara and I will go straight through here, Dear, you take the middle area and Steve can take the far end, okay?"

"Mommy," Tara whispered. "I know where Tommy is."

"You what?" her mother asked. "How do you know this?"

Everyone listened as Tara explained that when she had been picking blueberries with her mother the previous summer, she had seen Tommy crawl into a small opening under some blueberry bushes. When she and her mother had gotten closer to the place, she had gotten down on her knees and crawled in far enough to hear Tommy humming to himself somewhere where she couldn't see. The place felt too creepy for her to crawl in any farther but she remembered where it was and made plans to crawl into it even further when she was a little older and a lot braver.

With Tara leading the way, the Tuppencethalers made their way through the blueberry bushes and across the empty irrigation ditch to the far side of the farm. It wasn't long before Tara stopped and pointed to what looked like an impenetrable wall of thick foliage.

"There," she said. "He's in there. I just know it."

Everybody immediately started yelling, "Tommy!" "Tommy!" "Come out!" "It's time to go home:" "We know you're in there!"

There was no response.

They shouted again with the same result.

"Are you sure this is the place?" Steve asked.

"Yes," Tara replied. "I'll go and get him."

Before anyone could stop her, she ran to the edge of the brush, dropped to her knees, and disappeared just like Alice when she fell into the rabbit hole and landed in Wonderland.

The small crawlspace still felt creepy but Tara was older and braver than before so, after pausing for a moment to take a deep breath, she moved deeper into the thicket.

Several minutes later, Tara popped out of the bushes like a piece of toast popping out of a toaster.

"He's there," she said. "He asked me to give you a message."

Nobody said anything so Tara didn't say anything, either.

"Well?" Steve broke the silence. "What's the message?"

"Tommy wants me to tell you that you should go home and leave him alone. He says he won't starve because of all the berries."

Tommy's mother and father looked at each other, each hoping that the other was going to come up with a plan.

When nobody said anything, Steve asked, "Is that it? Did he say anything else?"

"Tommy wants me to tell you that he is a hot-stage."

There was more silence.

"He's in there by himself, right?" Steve asked.

"Yes." Tara replied.

Tara's mother asked, "Let me get this straight. He's in there by himself and says that he's a *hos*-tage?"

"No," Tara declared with certainty in her voice. "He said he is a *hot*-stage . . . whatever that is."

"Can you go back in and ask him who's holding him . . . uh . . . hotstage?" his father asked. "I'd do it myself but I think I'm too big to fit through the hole."

Tara disappeared into the hole and then popped out again.

"Tommy says that nobody is holding him. He doesn't understand the question. There's nobody in there to hold him except himself."

Tommy's mother spoke next, "I think Tommy means that he's holding himself hostage. Maybe he wants us to do something before he'll come out."

"Like having demands?" Steve asked.

Tommy's father had calmed down considerably and was even beginning to find some humor in the situation.

"Tara," he asked with a hint of amusement in his voice. "Would you please crawl back in and ask Tommy what his demands are for his release?"

Tara looked confused.

"You want me to ask him, 'What the demons are for . . . for his relief?'"

"Yes," her father said with a smile that was growing bigger by the second. "Something like that."

79

After Tara got the question straight, she vanished and reappeared once again.

"Tommy says he doesn't know what 'demands" is but he says there are some things he wants before he'll come out."

Tommy's father burst out laughing.

"Dear!" Tommy's mother said sternly. "This isn't funny."

Steve looked at his mother and then looked at his father, wondering whose side he should take. After a moment, he started laughing, too.

"What's so funny?" Tara asked her mother with a puzzled look on her face.

"I'm not sure," she replied as she forced her lips into the shape of a small smile. "But I suppose laughing about this is better than being all angry and upset."

Tommy's father was now laughing so hard that he had to choke back tears before asking, "Tara, did Tommy tell you what he wants?"

"Yes." She said.

"Well?" Steve asked with a bemused smile of his own. "What does he want?

Tara looked as if she was trying to remember everything that Tommy had told her. When she had gotten it all clear in her mind, she began to talk.

"First," she said, looking at her parents, "Tommy wants you to be nicer to him. He says he's big now and you should treat him with more respeak . . . or repseck . . . something like that."

Tommy's father glanced at Tommy's mother and gave his shoulders a little shrug as if to say, *Maybe he has a point . . .*

"And," Tara continued, "Tommy doesn't want to wear Steve's old clothes any more. He wants new ones and he wants Steve to be nicer to him, too."

Steve turned to his mother and said, "I don't get it . . . I'm not mean to him . . ."

"Steve," said his mother, "that's not the point. It's not about what you *aren't*. It's about what he wants you *to be*. He wants you to *be* nice . . . to be nice to him . . . or to be with him . . . something . . . anything. I think he wants a brother and you're the only one he's got."

"Thank you, Tara," said her father. "You've been a big help."

"Dad," Tara said. "There's one more thing Tommy wanted."

"What was that?" he asked.

"He . . . he wanted me to tell him that he's cute. I don't know why, but that's what he wanted so I said, 'Tommy, you're cute,' and he had me say it two more times before he let me leave."

"Do you really think he's cute?" Steve asked, hoping that the question would make her mad.

Instead of getting angry, Tara bent her head back, looked up at him straight in the eye, and in a quiet, calm, and measured voice, said, "Shut up, Steve!"

This time Tara's mother burst out laughing.

Steve didn't know what to say or do so he pulled out his cell phone and ear buds and started walking back towards the car. After only a few steps, however, he stuffed everything back into his pocket and stood as unmoving as a statue. After a moment, he turned around and walked back until he was standing in front of Tara.

He got down on his knees so he could put his face as close to hers as possible, and said, "Tara, you're right. I was a jerk. I'm sorry. I'll try to be a nicer brother for you, too."

This time no one laughed and it was Tara's turn to have no idea what to say or do.

"I love you, Tara," Steve said as he wrapped his arms around her with a hug.

"I love you, too," Tara said.

After the moment was over, Tara mother said, "What do we do now?"

"I think," said her father, "that Tara should go back to Tommy and tell him that we agree with his . . . his . . . the things that he wants."

"Okay," Tara said, but before she turned to leave, she looked at Steve and smiled.

Soon Tara came crawling out of the bushes, followed by a very blue-looking seven year-old boy carrying a half-empty can of blueberries in one hand and a stick in the other.

When they came closer, Steve asked, "What's the stick for?"

"It's a sword to fight pirates with," Tommy replied slowly, not knowing whether he was going to be yelled at or not.

When he realized that no one was yelling at him, he added, "I'm an Indian!"

"So you are," said his father proudly. "And the bravest brave I ever saw!"

Tommy's mother was not so enthusiastic.

"Just look at you!" she said with a touch of disgust creeping into her voice.

She was going to add, "I told you not to get blueberry juice all over your clothes . . . and just look at your face!" but she stopped in mid-sentence long enough to change course.

"Just look at you!" she repeated.

After a pause, she smiled and added, "You're beautiful!"

She bent over and gave him the biggest hug she could give, not caring if the blueberries stained her own clothes.

Tommy's father didn't say anything else but he did step in line so he could give Tommy a hug when his mother was finished with hers.

When the hug with Tommy's father was over Tommy stood quietly, staring at his father's hands.

After a long pause, he declared, "You don't have a hook."

Tommy's father had no idea what he meant by this, but Tommy knew.

It meant it was time to go home.

Buried Treasure

The sum total of Ruth's life consisted of five years growing up followed by twenty years in school, twenty years raising two children, and twenty years teaching nursing at a community college in Oregon. When she and husband, Sim, turned sixty-five years old, they retired from their jobs and decided to move to Seaview, Washington, where they planned to spend the rest of their lives as close to the beach as possible.

After a great deal of searching and researching, they bought a remodeled beach house built by a Columbia River steamboat captain in 1887. The house was small but with enough room for children and grandchildren to stay whenever they had time to come by for a visit.

Everything was perfect except for two things.

The first thing was that back when the riverboat captain built the house, it was just across the street from the beach. Over the years, the flow of river sand from the Columbia River had increasingly drifted north, creating Benson's Beach, filling in Beard's Hollow and moving the shoreline of the 27-mile Long Beach Peninsula to the west by nearly a quarter mile. Although everyone in Seaview still referred to the old

85

houses as "beach homes," it was now a good fifteen- minute walk to get to the water. Even so, the sound of the surf at night was sometimes so loud that it kept Ruth and Sim awake until, like a white-noise lullaby from Mother Nature, it rocked them to sleep like babies in a cradle.

The second thing that didn't turn out to be perfect was three months after they moved into their new home Sim dropped dead from a heart attack.

As Ruth recalled, "Sim got out of bed at three in the morning, said, 'I don't feel well,' walked into the bathroom and never came back out."

There was more to the story than that, of course, but because the longer versions usually ended up with Ruth fighting back tears, she opted for the abridged edition whenever the occasion permitted.

After Sim's death, Ruth's first impulse was to sell the house and move back to central Oregon where she could be closer to her two children and four grandchildren. But the friendly, small town atmosphere of her new home and a few budding friendships with women she met at the Presbyterian church convinced her to stay put and make the best of whatever life she had left.

Several months later, after a few dozen long, lonely walks to the beach, Ruth decided that if she was going to find any pleasure in these walks there would have to be more to them than just the walking. So she tried flying kites on the beach, she tried biking along the paved Discovery Trail, and she tried painting *plein air* watercolors on an easel set up on the Long Beach Boardwalk. None of it brought the excitement or satisfaction she was looking for.

She found herself spending more and more time alone in the house, baking cookies and putting them in the freezer so she could thaw them when her family came to town. As it turned out, she not only baked the cookies and froze them, but she also started eating them. She ate so many cookies that she gained ten pounds in two months.

When her oldest daughter returned home to Corvallis after a weekend visit to see her mother at the beach, she texted, *Mom, you've got to find a hobby or volunteer with the Food4Kids backpack thing you were telling me about. Join the art association. Do something . . . anything. If you don't get out of the house you'll die there, just like Dad, and I don't want that to happen. I love you and I want your great-grandchildren to meet you some day.*

Ruth immediately texted back, *I've tried. It's so hard without your father. But you're right. I'll keep trying. Thanks for the visit. I love you, too. Mom.*

Later that evening, an advertisement on the back of an old magazine changed Ruth's life forever.

Even before she finished reading the opening sentence, something began to stir in the depths of her soul. If she had tried to describe the feeling, she would have said it was like a sweet fruit bursting forth from a tree blossom, or a butterfly emerging from a cocoon, or like Jesus might have felt when he rose from the dead and walked out of the tomb alive. The excitement was tangible—an increase in her pulse, a widening of her pupils, and the twitching of her fingers—each of them eager to punch the toll-free number into her cell phone.

It was the sort of feeling she would have expected to have if she signed up with an on-line dating service or made a reservation on a cruise to some exotic destination. Instead, to her complete surprise, the thing that gave her the adrenaline rush was an ad for a metal detector.

"Discovery Detectors" *are solidly-built from durable, light-weight materials and state-of-the-art electronic components guaranteed to locate metallic objects the size of a B-B up to six inches underground, and larger metal objects up to six feet deep or more.*

She was hooked.

Her fingers did the walking and ten days later, a box arrived in the mail.

Because of the electronic components and pre-installed wiring, the unit required only a minimal amount of assembly before Ruth found herself slipping in the alkaline batteries and flipping the "ON" switch. She started swinging the detector around her living room and up against all kinds of metal objects but nothing happened. There were no beeps, no buzzes, and nothing lit up on the digital display.

Ruth turned the switch to "OFF" and sat down in her recliner with a thump, wondering if the thing was broken or defective.

Or, she thought, *maybe I should read the owner's manual . . .*

After reading the instructions through Step 3, she turned the detector back on. Her brain was immediately scorched by a loud, unyielding, high-pitched, ear-piercing shriek accompanied by a pyrotechnic digital display that suggested her sub-carpet flooring had been put in place with a hundred-thousand nails.

This might be trickier than I thought, she sighed as she flipped the switch back to "OFF."

This time she sat down and read the entire manual from cover to cover. She didn't stop until she understood the basic settings (including how to adjust the sound volume) and figured out how to interpret the information that showed up on the display.

After some trial and error practice inside the house, Ruth flung open the front door and charged out onto her front lawn like General Pickett leading his cavalry across the fields of

Gettysburg. Fortunately, for Ruth, her foray proved to be more successful than Pickett's. For every six or ten steps she took, the detector signaled that it had sniffed out one or more buried pieces of metal

At first, she made a mental note as to the location of each spot, but when there came to be more spots than she could keep straight in her mind, she rushed back into the house to find something to use as markers. Soon the lawn was covered with wooden building blocks Ruth had grabbed from the toy box she kept for the grandchildren.

As she searched, she came up with a system: Large blocks for the larger beeps and stacked blocks for the deeper locations. When she ran out of blocks, she turned off the metal detector, laid it gently against a tree and headed off to the storage shed to grab a shovel, a trowel and a bucket.

By the time it became too dark to see what she was doing she had dug seventeen holes and found four rusty nails, three rusty screws, the rusting haft from an old screwdriver, a small, tangled ball of rusty wire, and five small, unidentifiable or otherwise nondescript pieces of metal—all rusty.

Ruth, of course, was ecstatic.

"Eureka!" She shouted to no one in particular.

Sooner or later, she continued silently to herself, *I'm going to find something* . . . she paused for a moment trying to find the right word . . . *something really cool! That's the word . . . "Really Cool!"*

The next morning, Ruth's next-door neighbor Norm looked out his kitchen window and began speculating whether a spaceship containing a horde of extraterrestrial killer moles had landed on Ruth's property during the night and begun construction of a subterranean metropolis under her front lawn.

Some minutes later, when Ruth opened her front door and saw the lawn in the full light of day, all she could think was, *Oh, my . . . Sim would not be pleased with this at all.*

After putting as much of the dirt back in the holes as would fit, and after stomping down as much of the turf as she could salvage, Ruth sat down on her front steps and tried to decide where the metal detector should lead her next.

The number of possibilities was daunting. To begin with, there were 27-miles of beach to scan and, running parallel to the beach, an equally long, but even wider stretch of grass-covered sand dunes. There were also plenty of vacant lots to consider. Some of them preserved vestiges of structures that had once stood on them while others appeared to be as undeveloped and pristine as they had been when Lewis and Clark arrived in the neighborhood back in 1805.

Hmmm, she pondered, as she scratched her head with a new thought. *Back then, the beach would have been right across the street . . .*

Hmmm, she pondered some more, *in 1805 my house might have been actually sitting* <u>on</u> *the beach! Maybe Clark dropped something nearby when he walked up the coast and carved his name on a tree three miles north of here . . .*

Her musings continued.

. . . and there were all those shipwrecks. There's a name for that around here . . . what do they call it . . .?

Since the question was not rhetorical, she continued to ponder until she recalled the answer, which is, of course: "The Graveyard of the Pacific."

That led her to consider the possibility that an old shipwreck could have washed up in what was now her backyard.

It could have been a Spanish galleon, she mused with a smile forming on her lips. *A treasure ship filled with gold!*

90

For a fleeting moment, her eyes sparkled as they took on the reflection of ancient sea chests overflowing with jewels and doubloons.

After the feeling of euphoria had passed, Ruth sighed a sigh of epic proportions and her smile inverted itself into a sad sort of frown.

Whom am I kidding? She said to herself. *I'll be lucky if I ever find a plugged nickel.*

With that thought, her eyes dulled as they took on the reflection of old coffee cans filled with rusty nails.

She closed her eyes, straining to hold back the tears that were beginning to rise up from some place deep inside.

Sadness and grief settled over her like smog as she recalled the day she and Sim had spotted the "For Sale" sign on that very lawn. The house behind the sign was exactly what they had been looking for. They called the real estate agent, and within the hour they had made an offer—an offer accepted by noon the following day.

Ruth still had the house but she no longer had Sim to share it . . . and now she had gone and dug up Sim's lawn . . . his beautiful lawn!

Despite her best efforts to hold them in, Ruth's tears were not to be denied. They flowed freely down her cheeks and she began sobbing. Time stood still as memories of what had been came crashing head-on with hopes and dreams that would never be.

When the sobbing stopped and the flow of tears had slowed to a trickle, she was left with the feeling of being profoundly alone.

Her heart cried out the words of Psalm 22, the same words Jesus had spoken from the cross, *My God! My God! Why have you forsaken me?*

Although the thought was expressed as more of scream than a prayer she found herself adding the words, *Help me, God . . . please . . . help me . . .*

As soon as the prayer was over she sensed a presence hovering next to her and felt the touch of a comforting hand on her shoulder . . . just the way Sim used to touch her when she . . .

"Ruth?"

The word startled her. Although it was spoken in a whisper, it was spoken loudly and clearly enough to cause her head to snap up and her mind to snap awake as if from a deep sleep.

Before she could open her eyes, the word came to her a second time.

"Ruth? Are you all right?"

She turned her head and opened her eyes. It was Norm.

"Am I what?" she stammered, unsure why he was there and what he had seen. "I mean, no, I'm all right . . . I mean, yes, I'm . . ."

She could tell she wasn't making a whole lot of sense so she stopped in mid-sentence, lowered her eyes and waited for Norm to make the next move.

"I saw your lawn when I looked out my window this morning," Norm said as he sat down next to her on the steps. "Did you lose something?"

My husband, you dumb ass, she mumbled angrily to herself as the tears began to reappear. *I lost my damn husband!*

As angry as she was, the tears never got a second chance to show up. The reason for this was that instead of crying, Ruth started laughing.

She laughed because she realized how mean she was feeling towards a kind and caring 80-year old neighbor she knew had lost his own spouse two years earlier. She laughed because she realized that although Norm's voice was serious and comforting, his face was lit up with an impossibly incongruous smile. And she laughed because she realized that the thought of digging up her front lawn to find her lost husband was . . . well . . . it was funny . . . laugh-out-loud funny.

When she stopped laughing, Norm asked the obvious question, "What's so funny?"

"Life," Ruth replied with her smile as wide as Norm's. "Sometimes it doesn't make a whole lot of sense."

As far as Norm was concerned, life made a great deal of sense, but he could tell that Ruth had suddenly shifted gears from bad to better and didn't feel this was the time to start a debate on the subject.

Instead, he nodded his head, emitted a small grunt, put his arm around Ruth's shoulders and said, "Let's go get a cup of coffee. You can drive."

They spent the next hour at the Long Beach Coffee Roasters while Ruth talked about Sim, about cookies, about her family and, of course, about her metal detector. Norm spent the hour listening to Ruth, sipping his coffee, uttering small grunts and nodding his head every so often. The head nodding was intended to show empathy, to encourage Ruth to keep talking and, no less important, to keep his circulation moving and his arthritic spine from fossilizing.

Ruth never got around to drinking her coffee, but on the drive home, she invited Norm over to her place for dinner.

"It's been a while since I had home cooking," he said. "I mean other than the food I cook for myself. I guess that's home cooking, but it's not the same as when Peggy was . . . well . . . you know . . . doing the cooking."

He paused for a moment before remembering that Ruth had asked a question that needed an answer.

"Yes," he said as Ruth pulled into her driveway. "Dinner sounds nice. I'll bring a bottle of wine. We can raise a toast to *l'chaim!*"

"To life!" Ruth echoed with a smile "Even if it doesn't make a whole lot of sense."

As Norm stepped out of the car and began heading towards his house, Ruth added, "Thanks for the coffee . . . although I didn't drink any of it . . . I talked the whole time . . . I'm so sorry . . . next time you can do the talking, okay?"

Norm stopped, turned, and with a smile, replied with his patented grunt and nod.

Ruth added, "Dinner is at 6:00. I'll see you then."

"I'll be there," Norm replied.

At 6:00, the salad was green, the wine was red, the roast was tender, and the dessert, of course, was cookies.

At this point in the story, it is tempting to say that despite their fifteen-year age difference, Norm and Ruth fell in love, got married, and lived happily ever after. Tempting, perhaps, but since there is a well-known prayer that includes the phrase, "Lead us not into temptation," it is probably best to simply stick with the truth and leave the fairy tales to the Grimm Brothers. In any case, depending on how you look at it, things turned out to be just as interesting or maybe more so, than anything Jacob or Wilhelm might have dreamed up.

What happened was that Ruth and Norm agreed to have dinner once each week—on Tuesdays, if you really need to know. They took turns hosting and became dear friends who kept an eye on each other when they were at home and the other eye on each other's property when one of them was away.

As the weeks went by, Ruth became more involved in her church and spent an hour or two each Thursday morning helping with the Food4Kids backpack program. She got so busy that she tucked the metal detector in the guest room closet and completely forgot about it until Thanksgiving came along and her oldest granddaughter spotted it, dragged it out into the living room and asked Grandma what it was.

"It's an electro-magnetic device that detects the presence of certain kinds of metal that would otherwise be concealed under the ground," she explained.

Ruth's six-year old granddaughter stared at her blankly.

"Let me put it this way," Ruth tried again, "it's like a magic wand that you wave over the ground and it tells you what's buried there."

"Oh," her granddaughter replied, adding, "Thanks, Grandma," as she skipped away to search out something more in tune with the interests of a six-year old girl.

As Ruth returned the detector back to the closet, she began to feel the old stirring again. Out of curiosity, she flipped the "ON" switch and was surprised to find that the original batteries were still working.

Maybe I'll take it for a little spin when everyone leaves, she thought.

On Monday morning when the house was empty of guests, a Pacific storm blew in carrying heavy rain and wind gusts that registered over 90 miles an hour at Cape Disappointment. In Seaview, the gusts only reached 71 mph but that was enough to shear off the top of a forty-foot Sitka Spruce in Ruth's front yard.

On Tuesday morning, Norm was kind enough to carve the debris up with a chainsaw. He kept the larger pieces for firewood and tossed the rest into the back of his pickup to haul to the dump.

"Let's go," he said, waving Ruth towards the truck.

"Go where?" she asked with a smile.

"To the place where TVs and tree branches go when they die," he replied with a smile of his own.

As they turned left from Sid Snyder Dr. onto Sandridge Road, Ruth pointed to a crumpled structure on one of the corner lots.

"Looks like the wind took that down, too," she said. "It was still standing when Sim and I moved here in May."

"It's been there as long as I can remember," Norm added.

"What was it?" Ruth asked. "A barn?"

"Well," Norm replied, "back when I first moved here it was where folks went to buy meat."

"You mean, like the butcher?"

"Yes, I guess you could call it that. There wasn't a supermarket back then, and if you needed some meat, this is where you'd come and get it."

The rest of the drive was uneventful, which is not surprising seeing how Ruth wasn't paying much attention to it. She spent most of the time daydreaming about what might be lying under the ruined butcher shop and under the ground it stood on. Of all the vacant lots she had seen, this one seemed the most likely to turn up something "really cool."

That afternoon she tracked down the owner of the property, a man named Ben who turned out to be someone she knew from church.

After some small talk about the property, Ruth cut to the chase and asked, "Ben, do you mind if I snoop around with a metal detector.

"Be my guest," he told her. "If you find anything valuable give me 25% and we'll call it as square as a meal."

"Or as square as a deal," she replied.

Wednesday morning, bright and early, Ruth and Norm pulled the metal detector out of the back of the pickup and began a systematic sweep of the property. There seemed to be metal everywhere, both on top of the ground as well as under it.

"Too much of it," Ruth concluded. "It'll take forever to dig it all up."

"Looks like it," Norm agreed as he tapped his toe against an old wheel rim.

"Why don't you try over there?" he added, pointing to the far corner of the lot that seemed empty of any surface debris.

As Ruth searched the area, the detector fell as silent as a leaf falling from a tree.

"Nothing," she declared with a sigh.

Her conclusion was summarily withdrawn as the detector gave a low moan and registered something large nearby. In a matter of moments, Ruth found the exact spot.

"Something's down there," she declared. "Three or four feet down . . . unless it's something really large or dense. Then it could be deeper."

"'X' marks the spot," Norm said with a smile as he drew the letter in the dirt with his toe.

Since the Long Beach Peninsula is essentially little more than an enormous sand spit, digging in the ground did not turn out to be very difficult, even for 65-year old Ruth and 80-year old Norm.

About three feet down, however, the sand surrounding the hole gave way and refilled it.

"Keep digging," Norm said. "Just throw the sand further away so it doesn't come back to bite you."

At three and a-half feet, the shovel hit something solid. It was a chest; not a large chest, but a chest just the same, just large enough for a football to fit inside.

Neither Norm nor Ruth said a word as they bent over and lifted the surprisingly heavy box onto more solid ground. The padlock that secured the chest was still intact but the hinges on the other side had rusted through making it easy to open.

The space inside was taken up by a large leather bag that appeared to be remarkably intact. The leather was hard and stiff from age and the bag retained the shape of the box as they removed it and laid it on the ground. The words, "Bank of Ilwaco" were clearly visible where someone had once stenciled them on the bag.

The cord that secured the opening at the top of the bag broke into pieces as soon as Ruth touched it.

"So, how do we open it?" Ruth wondered. "The leather is as hard as a rock."

"Let me try," Norm said as he pulled a well-honed penknife from his pocket.

The blade cut a three-inch gash in the leather as easily as if it was cutting through paper.

When Ruth put her hand through the hole there was a dull clink of metal on metal.

What she pulled out of the bag was a 1926 silver dollar.

"Let's take it home and see what else is in there," Norm said.

"Wow!" Ruth said.

Back at Ruth's place, they counted ninety-seven silver dollars, twenty-seven half-dollars, thirty-two quarters, fifteen $5 gold coins, twenty-five $10 gold coins and ten $20 gold coins.

Although Ruth took a great interest in the matter, she never did find out where the money had come from or why someone might have buried it. Since the most recent coin was dated 1929 her guess was that it might have been related to the stock market crash of 1929 and the Great Depression that followed, but there was no way she could ever know for sure. Some mysteries, she decided, are fated to remain mysteries forever.

The value of the hoard was one mystery that didn't remain one for very long. A little math showed that the face value of the coins was $643.50 and a little research on the internet revealed that the meltdown value of the gold and silver was $30,000 and the numismatic value of the coins for collectors was somewhere over $40,000.

Just like Ruth said . . . "Wow!"

After dividing the coins according to their individual value, Ruth gave a fourth of them to Ben and offered Norm half of the rest.

"No thanks," he told her. "All I need is a loaf of bread, a bottle of wine, and . . . a home-cooked meal once a week!"

Ruth donated 10% of her windfall to the church as a thank offering and, after giving it some thought and talking it over with her daughters, she accepted Ben's invitation to drive with him to Astoria for dinner followed by a concert at the Liberty Theater.

It turned out that Ben, a 68-year old widower, had been just as lonely as Ruth. The two of them hit it off immediately, fell in love, got married six months later, and invited Norm over for dinner every Tuesday night for as long as he lived, which turned out to be a very long time!

Ruth lost the ten pounds she had gained and lived long enough to hold four great-grandchildren on her lap at the same time.

The metal detector went back in the closet until her oldest granddaughter turned twelve years old and decided that searching for gold might be a great way to meet boys. She found the detector under her Christmas tree in Corvallis the following December and, that same afternoon, took it to a nearby park and met the boy she later married.

It all goes to show that real life is sometimes as good as— or even better than fiction . . . and sometimes . . . well . . . it's hard to tell the difference!

Sunset & Evening Star

I am predisposed to motion sickness.

If I ride a rollercoaster, I will throw up.

If I try to read in a car when it is moving, I will throw up.

If I fly on an airplane, I will throw up.

If I take a weeklong cruise, I will throw up every hour of every day for a week.

Doctors have told me it's all in my head.

More precisely, they say there's something wrong with my inner ear. Maybe the fluid in my cochlea sloshes around the wrong way, or maybe my stirrup and anvil are misaligned, or maybe my Eustachian Tube has a kink in it. I guess I'm not smart enough to understand all the anatomical reasons for how my ear can tell my brain to start spinning around and my stomach to turn itself inside out, but that's the way it is.

It's like a curse, and when the nausea kicks in I might as well be demon possessed. It's that bad . . . really.

If it wasn't for a chemical compound called *Dimenhydrinate* I'd probably spend weekends and vacations sitting in a chair hoping the Pacific Plate wasn't deciding to take a sudden dip into the Subduction Zone off the Washington coast. Such an event would have the potential to cause an oceanic disturbance of a magnitude sufficient to create a tsunami large enough to sweep everything and everybody over and across the Long Beach Peninsula into Willapa Bay, which being an arm of the ocean, would also fill up and send water to meet us head on from the opposite direction. The possibility of a tsunami doesn't really worry me very much, but the thought of the ground moving under my feet terrifies me. The way I figure it, by the time the tsunami arrives I'll be feeling so sick to my stomach that I'll welcome it with a sigh of relief.

Dimenhydrinate, aka Dramamine, is what I use to keep the demons from taking full possession of my stomach. In pill form, this wonder drug allows me to fly on planes. As a patch behind the ear, it allows me to go on cruises. It is not, however, sufficient in any shape, form, or configuration to allow me to read a book in a moving car, ride a roller coaster, or to survive air turbulence or stormy seas without turning green.

I mention this because not long ago my friend Colin invited me to go salmon fishing with him and his friend Pete. He did this because he knows I love fishing.

The type of fishing I enjoy involves walking along high mountain lakes and streams with a fly pole. The kind of fishing Pete and Colin enjoy involves going out into the ocean in a small boat.

For some reason I haven't figured out yet, I said, "Sure I'll go, it sounds like fun. Thanks for the invitation!"

Pete's 22-foot salmon boat was moored at a temporary birth in Ilwaco harbor. It was a boat of the open-air variety meaning there was no roof on it. Without the motor, it would have looked like a larger version of the aluminum rowboat I used to paddle around in Lake Tahoe when I was a kid spending summers with my grandfather. It looked marginally big enough to venture out onto the Columbia River but nowhere near big enough to motor through the notoriously treacherous Columbia River Bar and out into the largest ocean on the face of the earth.

As I considered my options, an old Breton prayer crossed my mind. The prayer had been a favorite of President John F. Kennedy who kept an engraving of it on his Oval Office desk back in the days when he used to occupy the place. The prayer goes like this:

"O God, Thy sea is so great and my boat is so small."

The memory of Kennedy's PT 109 being cut in half by a Japanese ship during World War 2 did not offer me much consolation in the matter.

Neither did the recollection of Tennyson's well-known poem, *The Crossing of the Bar*, where he used the image as a simile for passing from life to death . . . or death to life, depending on how you read it. Until that moment, I had been fond of the poem but as I stepped into the boat and donned the prerequisite life jacket, the poem's sentiments did not strike me as being particularly comforting.

"What's the Bar Report this morning?" Colin asked.

Since I had no idea what he was talking about I assumed he was talking to Pete.

"Four to five feet at the moment," Pete replied, looking at me as if I was the one who had asked the question, "and the Buoy Reports suggest a good spacing between the swells. The tide's coming in so the river and the ocean will be calming each other down a bit. During an ebb tide, or when the waves crest more than eight feet, I don't even think about going out there in a boat this size. It's a beautiful morning and the tide won't turn for five more hours, so let's get going and bring some fish back before breakfast!"

It was 5:45 a.m. on a calm, cloudless morning in early June. I had set my alarm for 4:45 and had taken the recommended dose of my favorite antiemetic (plus one pill

103

extra "just in case") shortly before Pete and Colin arrived to pick me up. After reading that the "non-drowsy" version was a different compound and not as effective, I'd opted for the original version of the stuff. Given my concerns about losing my empty stomach over the side of the boat, falling asleep during our outing was the least of my worries.

It wasn't that I didn't trust Colin or Pete to take good care of me, it was the river and the ocean I didn't trust. Colin had explained to me earlier that Pete operated a charter fishing boat out of Ilwaco for nearly thirty years. He estimated he had crossed the bar over 8,000 times.

"When did he retire from the charter boat business?" I had asked.

"He didn't," Colin explained. "Someone ratted on him and he lost his license."

"What do you mean?"

Colin paused for a long time, as if trying to decide how much of the story to tell. In the end, he told as much of it as he could remember.

"Pete's boat, the *Sunset*, was licensed to carry twelve passengers, but one morning, when the spring Chinook were running thick and fast, thirteen people showed up—three more than had signed on for the trip. Pete knew his boat could hold fifteen people safely and he had enough life jackets for as many as twenty. He knew it was wrong to do, but he let them all get on anyway. They spent the morning surrounded by two hundred other fishing boats just upriver from the Megler Bridge.

"Marty Gaynor, one of Pete's old buddies who runs a charter boat named the *Evening Star*, had been holding a grudge against him over the placement of crab pots the previous winter. Marty accused Pete of running his pots too close to his own. Pete said that he had put them in the same place he had put them for twenty years but admitted there may have been some drift from a winter storm and some stronger than usual currents. For some reason, Marty didn't accept the explanation and threatened to cut the lines on all of Pete's pots if he ever did it again. Pete had apologized for the misunderstanding but Marty wouldn't even shake his hand on it. Months later, friends told Pete they had heard Marty swearing up and down that sooner or later he was going to get even.

"Marty was also out on the river that day and, for some reason—perhaps out of spite—counted the number of people on Pete's boat. He called the Washington State Fish & Game Department on his cell phone and reported the violation. Later that day, when Pete pulled into the harbor he was boarded by the state game warden who issued a citation and suspended his operating license.

"Pete admitted the mistake but took the issue to court to get his license back. Marty, however, testified that Pete had made the same "mistake" more times than he could count as a way to squeeze a little more money out of each trip. In his defense, Pete swore that he had never done it before and, in any case, he had only charged for the first twelve.

"The court ruled against Pete, increased his fine and took his charter license away permanently. Pete and Marty hadn't spoken to each other since. This was awkward because they lived within two blocks of each other in Seaview and were constantly running into each other at the store, in restaurants and at community events.

"The ruling," Colin explained, "devastated Pete, ruined his reputation and almost broke up his marriage. Most of his friends, including me, supported him through the ordeal but in the end, Pete sold the *Sunset*, gave up commercial fishing and crabbing, and took an early retirement.

"The only fishing he does now is for pleasure and the only reason he takes people like me with him is because he knows it's not safe to go out by himself.

"So," Colin added, "don't worry about the trip. Pete's the best there is. If I had any doubts, I wouldn't be going out with him myself."

As Pete's boat pulled out of the harbor the sun rose over the Columbia River.

Back in 1792 when Captain Gray sailed the *Columbia Rediviva* across the bar and became the first American to enter the river, the main channel ran along what is now the Washington State shore, along Baker Bay and Sand Island. When Oregon became a state in 1859, the boundary line separating it from Washington Territory was drawn along that original channel. This is why the "Welcome to Oregon" and "Welcome to Washington" signs are at the north end of the Megler Bridge. Because of shifting sand and the dredged relocation of the main channel to the Oregon side years later, the actual location of the state line along this stretch of the river is still up for grabs, with Sand Island currently claimed by both states.

Back before Gray made his river debut, Spanish ships made frequent forays across the bar. Their preferred mooring was just alongside a small island that can still be seen between old Fort Canby and Ilwaco. When Lewis and Clark reached the Pacific in 1805, they hoped to find an American ship anchored there, waiting for them with supplies. Their hope was not realized, at least in that regard.

Fort Canby is now the site of the United States Coast Guard Station Cape Disappointment. As we motored past the spot, a slight breeze began to stir the otherwise smooth waters of the channel. After passing between Sand Island and Jetty "A", we turned west into the main channel of the Columbia River with the dramatic headlands of Cape Disappointment on our right. Built in 1856, the dramatically situated Cape Disappointment lighthouse is not only the oldest lighthouse in the Pacific Northwest, it is also the only lighthouse on the West Coast with a band painted around its middle.

The water of the Columbia River funnels into the Pacific Ocean between two massive stone jetties. The South Jetty was completed in 1895 and extended to its present length of four and a-half miles in 1913. The North Jetty was completed in 1917 and is two and a-quarter miles long. Among other things, the construction of the jetties deepened the river channel, reconfigured the dangerous Clatsop Spit on the south and Peacock Spit on the north, and pushed the bar further out into the Pacific Ocean.

Even on a clear, windless day with a flood tide there was no doubt in my mind when we entered the area known as the Columbia River Bar. The river began to move and stir like a leviathan awaking from sleep. The water began to pile up in great swells, rising and falling in what seemed to be frightening randomness.

Pete, however, knew the choreography well enough to steer the boat between and around the deepest troughs and the highest peaks. Never before in my life had I been in such a small boat surrounded by such walls of water. I felt like Moses and the Israelites must have felt when they passed through the Red Sea with the water piled up on both their right and their left.

To my surprise, the combination of Pete's skill and Dramamine kept my stomach on an even keel even though the keel of our boat was more "odd" than "even" most of the time.

The dance through and across the Bar lasted about ten minutes with Pete constantly adjusting speed as he ran the boat like a knight zigzagging its way across a chess board.

Slowly we edged our way out of the channel and alongside the western end of the North Jetty where there seemed to be less turbulence. As we cleared the jetty Pete steered north across Peacock Spit with Benson's Beach, North Head Lighthouse and Beard's Hollow passing on our right. Soon we were half a mile out from the Seaview beach, surrounded by forty or fifty other boats. Most were our size but there were also larger boats with raised cabins and several that appeared to be charters.

Once we crossed the Bar, Colin kept busy rigging the poles. Slowly and deliberately, he attached a time-tested combination of swivels, leaders, flashers and hooks to the lines. As he pulled the herring bait out of the cooler, I could see that some had been dyed blue and some red.

"What's with the colors?" I asked. "I always figured fish were colorblind. Besides, if they're swimming beneath the bait they'll be looking up at the sky and all they'll see is a dark silhouette. I don't get it, why the colors?"

Pete shrugged and all Colin could say was, "Sometimes they hit the red herring and some days they seem to prefer the blue. I really don't know why. It's just the way it is. Personally, I prefer the blue. Is that all right with you, Pete? If I go with the blue this morning?"

"Go for it," Pete said. "We're in a good spot; the water is thirty-five feet deep; and I've seen four boats pull in salmon since we've been talking."

The boat rocked slowly back and forth as the one to two-foot swells passed under us on the way to their foreordained encounter with the North American continent. The air was fresh, the wind was low and the only sound was the surf breaking on the beach, the squawk of gulls looking for a free meal, a symphony of boat motors and indecipherable fragments of distant conversations.

Colin let out a line and handed me the pole.

"Hold on tight," he said. "If you get a hit set the hook and keep the line tight. The rules require barbless hooks so you'll lose the fish if you don't keep it taut."

For over sixty years, I have fished for trout in the high Sierra, most of the time using a fly pole at elevations between 8,000 and 11,000 feet. At that altitude most Rainbows, Brookies, Brown Trout and Goldens are between seven to ten inches long with the occasional twelve or thirteen incher showing up on a good day. Aside from fly fishing, the largest fish I ever pulled in was a Mackinaw in Lake Tahoe. I remember my father once landing a nineteen pounder off of Logan Shoals, on the Nevada side of the lake near Cave Rock, but the largest I ever caught was around five or six pounds.

Today, however, I was fishing for salmon in the Pacific Ocean. As I held the pole, I felt cold chills run down my back as I viscerally experienced the thrill of anticipation. The feeling was exhilarating.

Colin finished rigging the other two poles and ran the lines out on both sides of the boat with mine in the middle. Pete slid his into a pole holder while he steered. Colin and I sat side by side at the back of the boat holding the poles in our hands.

"Keep the tip up," Colin reminded me.

As I lifted the pole, I felt a bump, a tug and a hard pull.

"I've got one!" I said.

"All right!" Colin said.

What followed was a long litany of directions and instructions on how and when to reel in, when to let the line run out, and how to adjust the amount of drag.

"I've got one, too," Pete said in a tone of voice that made it clear this was not the first time he had hooked a fish. "I'll hold it until you get that one in the boat."

It only took a few minutes to bring my fish alongside. Colin slid a net under the creature and hoisted it into the boat. As he did, the hook slid out of the salmon's mouth and tangled itself in the net.

"Nice catch," Colin said. "It's about eight pounds and it's a keeper."

"What do you mean, 'It's a keeper?'" I asked. "Is there a size limit or something?"

"No," he explained. "You have to let it go if it's a wild fish. We only get to keep hatchery salmon.

"See there?" he pointed to the back of the fish. "There's a little vestigial fin called the adipose fin . . . at least it would be there if this was a wild salmon. Before they release the hatchery fish into the river, they cut the fin off. If it's missing you can keep the fish. If not, you release it."

It was clear my salmon was not happy being out of the water insofar as it was doing all it could to flop around in the hopes of getting away. Colin ended its hopes by whacking it on the head with a small but heavy wooden club. Then, after untangling the hook from the net, he helped Pete land his salmon.

"Aw, shucks," Colin said, pointing at the small fin on the fish's back. "Go home to Mama," he added as he dropped the salmon back into the water.

Recreational anglers are allowed to keep two salmon per day. As it turned out, Pete and Colin each caught their limit and I had to settle for one.

"Don't feel bad," Colin said in an unnecessary attempt to console me, "I've got more salmon in my freezer than I know what to do with. You can have one of mine to take home. I'll even fillet them for you."

"Thanks, Colin," I said with a happy smile. "One salmon is plenty, but I won't argue if you want to give me one of yours! And thanks for doing the filleting. I've cleaned hundreds of fish but never one this size. I'd probably make a mess of it."

110

"8:15 and time to head back for breakfast," Pete exclaimed as Colin began taking down the poles.

As the boat made a u-turn south towards the river, I noticed the weather had changed. I had been so intent on trying to catch salmon that I hadn't paid attention to the wind picking up, the sky turning gray and the waves growing larger and choppier than they were when we started fishing.

Maybe it was because I suddenly felt the increased motion in the boat . . . Maybe it was because the effect of my magic pill was wearing off . . . Whatever the reason, my stomach began to go up when the boat went down and vice versa. It was not a pleasant feeling.

I reached into my pocket to take another pill or two but couldn't find the container anywhere.

Nuts, I groaned to myself. *I must have left them on the bathroom counter.*

Colin extended his hand in my direction. "Here's a granola bar to hold you over until we get breakfast," he said.

Maybe it was my increased anxiety . . . Maybe it was the thought and sight of food . . . Whatever the reason, I could feel my skin begin to turn the color of a chameleon sitting in a lime tree.

The next fifteen minutes found me preoccupied with my stomach as I tried every trick I could think of to keep it from exploding. I held my breath for long periods of time. I tried meditative techniques. I tried fixing my eyes on the horizon. I tried taking small sips of water. I tried staring at the North Head Lighthouse as it drifted past on our left.

The situation brought to mind the time I climbed 14,180 foot Mt. Shasta. A medical doctor who joined my group at Horse Camp suggested that to avoid altitude sickness I should nibble on food throughout the eight-hour trek. I consumed an amazing amount of trail mix that day and, like the doctor promised, I never once felt light-headed or queasy.

"Colin," I said, "I'll take the granola bar if you still have it."

"Here," he said. "*Bon apetit.*"

Desperate times demand desperate measures so even though it seemed counter-intuitive, I began nibbling on the granola bar.

I should have followed my intuition.

The first bite produced an effect similar to the cannon shot ski resorts use to trigger an avalanche. Cause and effect; What goes up must come down; Or, in my case, what went down must come up.

By the time we rounded the North Jetty and reentered the channel, I had coughed and retched myself into exhaustion.

"Cheer up," Colin said with a smile. "We're almost home."

His attempts at encouragement were undermined when he added, "Wow, look at the size of those waves!"

For some reason, the Bar had taken on the topography of the Himalayas, with K2s, Everests and Kanchenjungas, popping up and down like Whack-a-Moles on every side.

"Hang on tight," Pete shouted with what I felt was too much enthusiasm, "This is going to be fun"

Earlier that morning, on our way out, we had been moving in the direction of the flow of the river. Now, however, we were not only going against the current, but an unseasonably strong offshore wind had suddenly come up that piled the swells into peaks and blasted the crests into spray that fell on us like rain.

It was so terrifying I forgot to feel nauseous.

"Maybe we should wait it out and come in later," Colin suggested.

"No," Pete replied with a smile, "It's good. The Coast Guard hasn't issued a warning yet so it can't be more than we can handle."

Two minutes later the Coast Guard issued a small craft advisory for the Bar.

If theme parks could reproduce a similar upheaval in a controlled environment, thrill seekers with cast iron stomachs would travel long distances, stand in long lines and pay big bucks for the opportunity to undergo what I was experiencing for free. It was scary, it was thrilling, it was breathtaking but, unlike the world-class glamour rides at Six Flags, it was not going to be over in three minutes.

Like all experienced boatmen, Colin and Pete were not only taking care of our situation, they were also monitoring the progress of other boats attempting the crossing.

"Hey, Colin," Pete shouted, "keep your eye on that small open boat over there, back behind us towards the South Jetty. He doesn't look as if he knows what he's doing. He keeps getting pushed sideways like he's fishtailing. If he's not careful he'll go over in a second."

"Got it, Captain. Aye, aye and all that," Colin shouted back, trying to inject some levity into a situation that had suddenly morphed into a struggle for survival.

Pete's marine band radio crackled with questions and expressions of concern from boaters over the increasingly rough conditions on the Bar. Despite my growing anxiety, I found some comfort in recalling that the Coast Guard always has one or two people visually scanning the Bar with powerful binoculars from a watch station on the ocean side of the Cape Disappointment lighthouse. Once, during an open house at Fort Canby, I was given permission to look through those binoculars. Today—perhaps at that very moment—it was my turn to be seen "up close and personal" through those same lenses.

The swells had become so high that it was now impossible to see what was happening to other boats . . . except for those few breathtaking moments when we crested a massive, pulsating mound of water and paused for a dramatic moment before plunging into a trough on the other side.

Pete's radio crackled in a way I assumed meant someone was about to ask another question or offer more information about the status of the crossing. I couldn't have been more wrong.

"Man overboard. I repeat, Man overboard."

The words were chilling. Someone had just plunged into a nightmare and had pulled their companions into the emotional horror along with them. The voice, clearly on the edge of panic, continued:

"This is Marty Gaynor, Captain of the charter boat *Evening Star* out of Ilwaco. We're on the north edge of the Columbia ship channel about half-way down the North Jetty, due west from Cape Disappointment."

"Do you have a GPS reading?"

"Just a second . . . here it is . . . I'm tripping my EPIRB[1]."

"We'll have a boat on the way in minutes. If possible, hold your place and keep the person in sight until we get a crew on site to assist. Do not attempt a recovery under these conditions unless you are confident you can do it safely. If in doubt, wait for assistance."

"Roger that."

"Good God!" Pete shouted. "That's them to port, about fifty yards . . ."

Pete grabbed the radio mike, "*Evening Star*, I'm about fifty yards away and have visual. Do you need assistance? Over."

"Yes, we've lost contact with the person in the water . . . Damn!"

"*Evening Star*? Are you there?"

---

[1] Emergency Position Indicating Radio Beacon

"Yes, we're here. We reversed engines to hold our place and the engine's quit on us. Attempting to restart. We're adrift and cannot hold direction. We request immediate assistance. This is a 'Mayday.'"

As the conversation between Gaynor and the Coast Guard continued, Pete veered our boat to the left under full throttle, squeezing out every inch of skill and experience he possessed as he dodged between the swells.

"If he turns sideways he's a goner," Pete shouted as Colin and I considered the odds that we were going to be pitched into the water ourselves. "Keep your eyes out for someone in the water and let me know if you see anything."

Within seconds, we were close enough to the *Evening Star* to appreciate the danger she was facing.

"I'm going to pull alongside," Pete shouted into the radio, "and when I do, toss us a line. Tie your end to the bow and we'll try to straighten you out until the Coast Guard arrives."

"Roger that."

A rope appeared and landed ten feet short.

"Colin, use the gaff to snag it and pull in it . . ."

As Colin grabbed the short, hooked pole that Pete kept secured alongside the net and fishing poles, Pete expertly maneuvered the boat close enough to the rope for Colin to grab it.

"Got it!" Colin shouted.

"Secure it to the stern," Pete shouted back. "And be sure to tie it as tight as you can. It's going to be taking a lot of stress. Tell me when it's ready."

"Ready! Secured!" Colin yelled.

"God help us!" Pete screamed to no one in particular except, maybe, to God.

Pete headed our 22-foot open boat directly into the wind until the rope pulled taut with the helpless 40-foot charter.

I had read about boats being "tossed" by the wind and the waves, but I had never given much thought to what the words were attempting to describe until I suddenly found our boat airborne, thrown into the air by the rising and falling of the raging swells.

"Get your knife out," Pete shouted over his shoulder as he struggled to avoid the wall of water looming in front of him. "If I yell, 'Cut,' cut the rope. Okay?"

"Okay," Colin shouted as he pulled a hefty fillet knife out of the tackle box.

The situation reminded me of the late health and fitness guru Jack LaLanne, when he used to swim across San Francisco Bay while pulling a boat tied to his waist by a rope.

"O God," I prayed, "Thy sea is so great and my boat so small."

Slowly, ever so slowly, our boat moved forward, pulling the *Evening Star* behind us with its bow now facing the full blast of the wind and waves head on, but with less danger of being knocked sideways and foundering.

In ten minutes, a 29-foot Coast Guard Defender response boat arrived to begin searching for the person in the water, followed moments later by a 47-foot Coast Guard rescue vessel whose mission was to assist the helpless charter boat itself.

With the Coast Guard now in charge, Pete followed the directions that came through the radio until the order came to release the towline from our stern.

"Cut!" Pete yelled.

As Colin's blade sliced through the rope, our boat, now freed from its burden, shot forward with a burst of speed and slid deep into a trough. Pete cut the throttle to regain control, but then quickly accelerated and banked into a u-turn, which pointed us towards safe harbor in Ilwaco.

Water sloshed in the bottom of our boat like bathwater, but fortunately, there was not enough of it for Colin or me to start bailing. Within minutes, we were out of the heavy turbulence and gliding past Buoy 11 through lowering swells.

A rescue helicopter from Coast Guard Air Station Astoria joined in the search and it was not long before a smoke bomb was dropped to guide the Defender to the point of rescue.

"Fifteen, maybe twenty minutes in the water," Pete announced as he glanced at his watch. "Unless he hit his head . . . or *her* head . . . he . . . or *she* . . .is probably going to be okay. I hope whoever it is realizes how lucky they are."

"They'd be a fool, not to," Colin replied, joining Pete in using a gender-neutral plural to split the difference. "And Marty's a fool if he doesn't realize how lucky he is to have you show up in the right place at the right time. Damn him to hell! If it hadn't been for the people on his boat I would have told you to leave him alone and let him sink."

"Yeah," Pete answered back, "the thought crossed my mind, too, but only for a second. I don't care who the person is, if they're in trouble on the water, and I'm in a boat close enough to help, then that's what I'll do."

Pete paused for a moment before adding, "I read this somewhere, I can't remember who said it, but it went sort of like this: 'If doing the right thing costs you big time . . . do the right thing anyway.' That's how I was brought up and that's how it's supposed to be. We did what we had to do."

Pete paused again before flashing a smile over his shoulder and saying, "Come to think of it, that was one heck of a ride, wasn't it?"

Colin nodded, and I might have joined him in expressing my agreement except for the fact that my body was so numb with adrenaline that I couldn't tell whether I was still nauseated or not.

After mooring the boat in Ilwaco, we decided to call it a day, skip breakfast and head home.

It was only 10:30 a.m., when Pete and Colin dropped me off at my house.

"Thanks for the adventure," I said lamely, not knowing what else to say.

"I'll bring the fillets over after lunch," Colin said before closing the car door. "That way you can cook them fresh or freeze them for later."

Colin was true to his word, and my wife whipped up a fresh-caught salmon dinner the following evening.

We later heard that the "man overboard" was, in fact, a man. Once back on shore, he was taken by ambulance to Ocean Beach Hospital in Ilwaco where, after being treated for exposure in the ER, he was released and sent home.

A week later, Pete bumped into Marty at Sid's Market.

There was an awkward, silent moment until Marty put out his hand.

There was another long, awkward moment until Pete reached out and gave Marty's hand an unenthusiastic shake.

"Thank you," Marty said.

Pete gave a slight nod of his head, and that was the end of it. So far as I know, they have not talked to each other since.

Several months later, the Coast Guard presented Pete with the Silver Lifesaving Medal; a civilian award given to a person "who rescues or endeavors to rescue any other person from drowning, shipwreck, or other perils of the water."

Pete didn't appreciate the fuss, but once the story had been detailed in the local newspaper, most folks forgot about it and turned their attention to other things.

For me, however, the experience remains as clear and vivid as the day it took place.

I continue to hold Pete and Colin in the highest respect for what they did that morning, and I am happy to report that they haven't invited me to go fishing with them since.

Bogged

Coleman McCrae and his wife, Bel, live on the south end of the Long Beach Peninsula in an old house surrounded on all sides by cranberry bogs. Cole inherited half of the bogs from his parents and grandparents, and the other half he either built from scratch or purchased from neighbors who, for one reason or another, wanted out of the cranberry business. Everyone who knows Cole knows he is a fanatic when it comes to cranberries. Both literally and figuratively, he eats and breathes cranberries.

Sunday through Saturday, dinner is at 6:00 p.m. sharp at the McCrae house. That is, of course, unless the cranberries require extra attention, in which case dinnertime has to stand in line and take its turn along with everything else.

During October and November, for example, the days are short but the hours are long as the bogs are flooded in preparation for the annual cranberry harvest. Machines called "beaters" move through the water knocking the berries off the vines so they float to the surface. The berries are corralled to the edge of the bog where they are sucked, or conveyed in a more gentle way, into the back of a truck. The truck goes to the local distribution center where the berries are weighed and packed before transported to a regional processing plant.

Most of the local growers are partners in the Ocean Spray national collective, a corporation where the growers are the shareholders. As far as cranberry production goes, Wisconsin produces half the national total with Massachusetts coming in second. Even though Washington State's crop is small in comparison, it is an important part of the local economy and a way of life for many families like the McCrae's.

Throughout the year, there is much to be done if a grower wants to produce the highest possible yield per acre. There is sand to replenish, fertilizer to be spread, pesticides to be sprayed, weeds to be eradicated, irrigation to be monitored, repairs to be made and, following the harvest each year, vines to be pruned and replanted where needed. It is more than a full-time job, especially for folks like Cole who has far too many bogs to handle by himself.

At 6:00 p.m., on what had been a rather forgettable Tuesday in January, Cole and his wife sat down to enjoy a slice of roast beef, a baked potato and a side salad garnished with a dollop of cranberries culled from their most recent harvest.

At 6:05 p.m., the phone rang.

With a groan and a sigh, Cole put down his fork, got up, walked across the kitchen and picked up the phone.

"Hello," he said, trying to sound more cheery than he felt, "this is Cole."

"Mr. McCrae, this is Marta. Where is Oscar? He isn't home. He was here for lunch and went back to work in the bogs and he didn't come back yet. He said he'd be home at 4:30 p.m. Do you know where he is? We were all going to drive to Astoria and go swimming this evening. It's not like him to be so late."

Cole could sense the anxiety in her voice but managed to squeeze in a wistful glance at his dinner before offering a few words of comfort and encouragement.

Oscar and Marta Castillo had been on Cole's payroll for nine years. Long before coming to the Peninsula, they had crossed the Mexican border with worker's visas. Those papers had been upgraded to green cards by the time Cole hired Oscar to help him maintain his fields and farm equipment. Prior to moving into their own home four years ago, they had rented one of the secondary houses that stood on the McRae's property.

The Castillos were a success story and Cole felt proud to have played a part in it. They had two school-age kids; the family spoke fluent English; and the parents were taking an on-line class in preparation for becoming naturalized citizens of the United States. Like most of the other Latino families on the Peninsula, the Castillos were good parents, active members of their church and in many other ways involved in their children's schools and the life of the local community. Cole considered Oscar, Marta and their kids to be part of his own extended family: a family that included the McCrae's own children and grandchildren, along with most of the other present and former employees who worked for him over the years.

"Well, Marta," Cole continued, "all I can say is that this morning, he was scalping the vines up at Bog 6. The weather's been so dry since harvest I figured we'd get the bog ready to go for those new vines I'm getting from MIT. I'm not sure what he was planning to do this afternoon. I assumed he'd be cleaning out the debris."

Cole stole another glance at his dinner and gave a small shrug of his shoulders in the direction of his wife before adding, "I'll tell you what, if you don't hear from Oscar in the next fifteen or twenty minutes call me back and I'll run out to see if I can find anything. It's almost dark, but I can take the truck. If you don't call back I won't worry about it, okay?"

"Fifteen minutes I call you back if Oscar not home. Thank you. Bye."

Fifteen minutes later—as Cole was savoring his last bite of beef and eying a plate filled with oven-fresh brownies—the phone rang a second time.

"Bel," he said as he hung up the phone and walked across the kitchen to where his winter coat and hat were hanging on a hook, "I'm going to take the truck up to Bog 6 and see if I can find out what happened to Oscar. I won't be gone long."

"Drive slowly, dear," Bel cautioned as he went out the door. "It's dark and . . ."

The door closed before she could finish the sentence.

Bel sighed and picked up a brownie. Before she could take a bite, the door re-opened and Cole added a word of caution of his own.

"Don't eat all the brownies while I'm gone!"

The door closed. Bel sighed again, and ate two brownies before covering the plate with cellophane and returning it to the table for Cole when he got back.

She didn't know it at the time, but the brownies were destined to sit there uneaten for a long time.

The McCrae's rectangular-shaped bogs lie close and tight together except where the dikes are wide enough for a truck or a tractor to drive between and around them. After every pair of bogs, there is an intersection where a vehicle can continue straight ahead or turn to the right or left depending on where the driver wants to go.

During the five-minute drive, Cole took note of the fading twilight to the west. If it wasn't for his headlights the bogs would have been shrouded in total darkness. As he pulled up to Bog 6, he saw a dark shape in the corner of the bog furthest from the driving path.

That's got to be the tractor, Cole thought to himself.

He stopped the truck and slowly backed it up at an angle until the twin lights shot across the bog like a pair of parallel laser beams.

"O God, no!" Cole shouted as he grabbed a flashlight. He hit the ground running as fast as his 70-year old legs and lungs could carry him.

"Oscar! Oscar!" he shouted as he made his way to the scalper and the overturned tractor that had been pulling it.

Even from eighty feet away he could see two legs sticking out from beneath the tractor. The sight hit him like a fist to his solar plexus. It knocked the air out of him and slowed his pace from a sprint to the cadence of a funeral march. The cold, mid-winter air suddenly felt hot on his cheeks. As he silently drew closer to the scene, he pulled his cell phone out of his pocket and absentmindedly began entering the numbers 9-1-1.

One hand held the phone to his ear while the other reached under the tractor and touched the hand of his friend, Oscar. The hand was as cold as death.

Cole shivered for a moment and then went numb, feeling neither hot nor cold . . . feeling nothing.

"Hello?"

The disembodied voice sounded far away and, at first, Cole was confused by it.

Why did someone say, "Hello?" he wondered. *Who would say something like that . . . now . . . out here . . .?*

"Hello? Can I help you?"

This time the voice sounded as clear and as close as the phone he was still holding to his ear.

"Yes," Cole said; his voice flat and expressionless. "You can help me. There has been an accident."

Cole knew that within minutes, the peaceful tranquility of his personal corner of paradise was going to be obliterated by wailing sirens, flashing lights, squawking walkie-talkies and the competing voices of first responders walking and running over, around and through his bogs.

Cole's first call had been to 9-1-1. His second call was to his on-site caretaker, Freddy Holmes, who lived less than 200 yards away in the house previously occupied by the Castillos.

"Freddy," Cole began as soon as Freddy picked up his phone, "There's been an accident at Bog 6. I've called 9-1-1. Everyone will probably take the short cut past your house to get here. You've got to stand in their way and have them park in front of the guest house. Put someone in charge so the road is clear for the ambulance. Find a way to guide the ambulance to the bog. The rest of them can walk."

As Cole paused to catch his breath, he put himself in Freddy's place and did his best to head off the question he knew was coming.

"It's Oscar," he said. "Get going or there's going to be a traffic jam that'll take all night to untangle."

"But what about . . ." Freddy began.

"Just do it, Freddy! Do it now!" Cole screamed.

You're panicking, he said to himself as the phone went dead. *You've got to get yourself under control. You've got to think . . . before they get here . . . what happened . . . how could it have happened?*

The question was already beginning to eat at him: "How could it have happened?" How could a tractor tip over in a bone-dry bog? Even if Oscar had caught a wheel in the drainage ditch that ran around the bog's perimeter it would have been unlikely the tractor would have tipped over . . . and even if it had, it would have fallen the other way . . .

Cole could hear the sound of sirens in the distance.

Maybe there was a soft place in the sand. Maybe the axle broke. Maybe Oscar had a stroke and turned the wheel too sharply as he collapsed. Maybe . . . Maybe . . . Maybe . . .

The word "Maybe" echoed in Cole's head until, a moment later, it was replaced by the sound of sirens converging onto his property like a swarm of angry bees.

A new thought replaced the previous ones in Cole's mind. He realized that in a matter of seconds, the bog would be trampled into oblivion. If there was anything on the ground worth looking at, he had better start looking now. But there wasn't enough time . . .

The same adrenaline that had pushed him to the edge of panic suddenly changed tune and delivered an overwhelming feeling of peace and calm. Time seemed to stand still as Cole pulled out his phone, opened the camera app and began to systematically walk around the area taking flash pictures of the ground, the tractor, the mower, and—although he hesitated before he could bring himself to do it—of Oscar.

His phone battery gave out just as two men rushed up, each carrying one of the two brightest flashlights that had ever had pointed in his direction. The light blinded him.

"Put those things down," he ordered with his hand covering his eyes. "Point them at the ground. I suppose you already know who I am. Who are you?"

It was Bob Wallace, the officer on duty that evening with the Long Beach Police Department and Russell Lundgren, the south county Sheriff's Deputy with Pacific County. Cole's bogs were located on both city and county land and the question of who had authority and jurisdiction over the situation was going to take some unraveling.

Fortunately, Bob and Russell had grown up on the Peninsula together and graduated from Ilwaco High School one year apart. Their friendship ran deep, and so did their commitment to the best interests of the community. Given the need to get an emergency situation under control, neither was inclined to waste time fighting a turf war.

127

"You take it, Bob," Russell said as they lowered their flashlights in deference to Cole.

"Okay," Bob replied. "We can sort it out later."

In the distance, Cole could see an ambulance slowly making its way between the bogs. He made a mental note to have Bel bake Freddy a batch of brownies as a "Thank you" for stepping up to the plate and hitting one out of the park on such short notice.

It occurred to him that there were not going to be any brownies for Oscar, and the thought of Oscar reminded him of Marta and their kids. There were not going to be any brownies for them, either, except perhaps, at the reception following Oscar's funeral . . .

Cole shook his head with a jerk, hoping to get his thoughts back on track.

"Marta," he muttered aloud to no one in particular. "Someone needs to call Marta . . . and someone needs to call Bel."

Cole knew it wasn't going to be him. For one thing, his phone was dead and, in any case, there were other matters that needed to be taken care of first. The calls would have to wait until later.

As the two officers got down on their knees and checked Oscar for signs of life, Cole saw two people jump out of the ambulance and begin sprinting across the bog. When the officers were done, they stood up and backed away to make room for the two EMTs who were already stepping forward with their emergency bags in hand.

"He's dead, Bonnie," Russell said to the first EMT to arrive. "But you'll need to confirm that yourself."

"Who is it, Cole?" Bonnie asked as she checked for a pulse.

"Oscar. Oscar Castillo," he replied.

As Cole spoke Oscar's name, he felt the full weight of the tragedy settle on his shoulders. Suddenly his knees felt weak and he looked for a place where he might sit. As he looked around the thought crossed his mind that there was going to be significant damage to the bog, damage that, come the next harvest, was going to negatively affect his bottom line. The thought shamed him. At a moment like this, money meant nothing. Oscar and his family, however, meant everything.

Instead of sitting, he walked over to Bob and Russell.

"What happened?" Bob asked.

"I don't know," Cole replied. "It was an accident, I guess. At least it looks like an accident. Oscar's wife—you know Marta, don't you? I think your son is the same age as their youngest boy, Alissandro . . . Anyway, Marta called this evening and asked me why Oscar was late coming home so I came out here to look and found him . . . pinned under the tractor . . . like this . . . I saw him scalping the bog this morning and Marta said he came home for lunch but that's all I know."

"This happened to my uncle in California," Russell said. "He didn't come home for dinner and my aunt found him under the tractor where it had slid down a ravine. A year later, she married her husband's brother . . ."

Russell's rambling was interrupted by Bonnie.

"He's dead so there's no hurry to move him. But the sooner Bob calls the Coroner, the sooner the body . . . I mean, Oscar . . . can be taken to the mortuary.

"By the way," Bonnie added, "any ideas on how to get him out from under the tractor? I'd hate to ruin the bog by bringing in heavy equipment to lift it off of him . . . "

"The bog doesn't matter," Cole replied. "Do what you have to do."

". . . or we could dig out some of the sand from under him," Bonnie continued, "and then pull him out. That would work."

Everyone agreed this would be the best plan.

"But first," Bonnie added, looking at Bob and Russell, "isn't there some investigation you're supposed to do before the Coroner gets here? You know . . . things like photographs and measurements?"

"Sure," Bob answered. "Even though it's a accident there has to be a report and we've got to get all the information . . . but it's late, and it's dark . . . the weather is good with no rain in the forecast . . . so I suggest we take a few pictures of Oscar before you pull him out. We'll close off the bog with yellow tape and take a better look at it in the morning. How does that sound to you, Russ?"

Russell nodded in agreement. He and Bob each snapped a few pictures and cordoned off the bog with yellow tape. When they were finished, everybody waited until Don Milner, the south country Assistant Coroner and owner of the local mortuary, arrived. With his consent, Freddy and a few of the volunteer responders who were standing around with nothing to do dug out the sand from under Oscar. Bonnie and her partner slid him out, put him on a stretcher and carried him to the Coroner's van. A minute later, the van drove off, taking the body to the mortuary for safekeeping until an autopsy could be set up in Longview.

By 8:15 p.m., everyone had left except for Bob, Cole and Freddy. When Bob offered to break the news to Marta, Cole said he wanted to go, too.

"Don't bother, she already knows."

The voice was Bel's.

The startled men turned and saw her standing only six feet away. Standing next to her was Marta.

130

The moment Bel heard sirens she had thrown on her jacket, stepped out of the house and walked over to see what was going on. As she stood to the side, unnoticed and out of the way, her phone rang. It was Marta, who had driven over to look for Oscar. There were so many cars that she had to park on the main road and start walking. She guessed immediately that the excitement had something to do with Oscar and, not knowing what else to do, she phoned Bel. They quickly found each other and spent the rest of the time standing or sitting together at the side of the bog watching the tragedy unfold.

Throughout the ordeal, Marta never expressed a desire to go over to where Oscar's body was lying. Instead, she simply watched from a distance and quietly cried until she ran out of tears.

"He was a good man," she said to no one in particular. "He was a good husband and a good father."

When her brief soliloquy was over, Marta turned to Bel and said, "I must go home now. I must tell the children. Somehow, I must tell the children."

"I'll go with you and spend the night," Bel said.

Cole had never been one to give people hugs but on this one night, for Marta, he made an exception.

After the hug, he turned and gave Bel a kiss on her cheek.

"Thank you," he whispered. "Call me when you're ready to come home. I've got some thinking to do. Something about this doesn't make sense."

Bel replied with a nod. Then, with their arms around each other, the two women headed off into the darkness along with Freddy, who offered to walk them to Marta's car.

Officer Bob followed a few steps behind, hoping that the rest of his shift would be free of interruptions so he would have time to write the first draft of his report.

As Cole climbed into his truck, he noticed the headlights had dimmed to a dull glow. With a sigh of relief, he managed to coax enough juice out of the battery to get the engine started.

Something else to take care of in the morning, he figured.

When he got home, the first thing he noticed was the plate of brownies sitting on the kitchen table. He didn't give them a second look.

Not long after, Bel sat in Oscar's recliner and listened quietly as Marta, surrounded by her children on the sofa, explained why their father was not coming home. There was some sniffling and a few simple questions followed by a prolonged and very uncomfortable silence. Marta broke the silence by asking if the children wanted to climb into bed with her and, when they all said, "Yes," they stood up and disappeared into Marta's bedroom.

Thirty minutes later, Marta returned to the living room, sat down on the sofa and motioned for Bel to sit next to her. They wrapped their arms around each other and, five minutes later, Marta was sleeping as soundly as the children. Bel gently covered her with a blanket from one of the children's beds and then, not knowing what else to do, sat down in Oscar's chair, leaned back and closed her eyes.

As she drifted back and forth between waking and sleeping her mind kept returning to Cole's parting words, "Something about this doesn't make any sense."

She did not sleep as well as Marta.

Cole, on the other hand, spent the evening with his cell phone plugged into his computer.

After charging his phone long enough to make it operational, he downloaded the pictures and began searching them for clues. Before he fell asleep with his head on his desk, he noticed two things.

The first thing he noticed was clear and unequivocal. According to the pictures, the tractor and scalper had moved across the bog in a straight line. The tires had not slipped into the drainage ditch, they had not caught the embankment at the edge of the bog, and they had not sunk into a soft spot in the sand. At no time had the tractor's front tires been turned to the right or to the left, at least not while they had still been on the ground. After coming to a complete stop, the tractor, with the scalper still attached, had, for no apparent reason, fallen over on its side. This led to a second mystery: if Oscar had been sitting in the tractor's seat when it tipped over Cole would have expected him to have either stayed there or been thrown out and away from the tractor when it hit the ground. Oscar's body, of course, was lying underneath the fallen tractor. The way Cole saw it, the only way this could have happened was if Oscar had already been lying on the ground when the tractor tipped over.

As he had said to Bel, "There's something about this that doesn't make any sense."

The second thing he noticed in the photographs was more ambiguous. On the floor of the bog—in an area where he had not yet taken a step—footprints seemed to come up to the edge of the fallen tractor, stop, shuffle a bit, and then head back the way they had come. It appeared as if the footprints had been made *after* the tractor had fallen over. Cole calculated that if the footprints continued in a straight line, they would intersect the dike on the south edge of the bog at a point approximately fifty feet past where the ambulance had parked earlier that evening.

The whole thing was like one of the jigsaw puzzles Bel was always working on. There were lots of pieces to choose from but so far, at least, they didn't seem to be fitting together very well.

I don't even know what the picture is supposed to look like, he yawned wearily.

Cole's eyes closed and his head began to sag. As his forehead softy came to rest on the desk, it occurred to him that if Oscar hadn't been scalping that section of the bog, the footprints would have been completely hidden amongst the untrimmed vines.

Part 2

Like most folks who live on a farm, Cole is an early riser; so when the phone rang at 7:00 a.m. the next morning he was not only awake, but he had already shaved, changed into clean clothes and was half-way through his first cup of coffee.

The phone call was from Officer Bob Wallace.

"Morning, Cole," he said. "It's been a long night and I'm not going to be able to keep awake much longer. I've got Chief Jacobson with me. Now that it's light enough, we're going to take a closer look at the bog so I can finish my report. If you're free, can you meet us there in ten minutes?"

"I'll be there," Cole replied. "As a matter of fact, I've cleared my calendar. I'm not going anywhere or doing anything until I figure out what happened to Oscar."

To his pleasant surprise, Cole's truck started up without any hesitation.

Once less thing to do this morning, he nodded to himself.

Before putting the truck into gear, he called Freddy and asked him to join them.

"I need you to know what's going on," he told him, "and I need to ask you a few questions about yesterday and what happened to Oscar."

"Sure thing, boss," Freddy said. "I'll see you in five."

After everyone shook hands and said, "Good morning" to each other, Chief Jacobson asked, "Well, Cole, how's Marta doing? Have you heard anything?"

"Nothing yet, Jake, I haven't heard anything from Bel so I suppose she's still at Marta's place trying to be of help. This whole thing bothers me. I mean, Oscar's dead, and that bothers me a lot, but that's not what I mean. I mean . . . what I mean is, I don't think that what happened was an accident. I took some pictures last night before Bob and everyone else showed up. Before you start checking things over this morning, I want to show you what I found."

After Cole, Freddy and the two police officers stepped into the bog, Cole showed how the tire marks ran in a straight line and how there was no logical explanation for how or why the tractor had fallen over. He then explained why it didn't make sense that Oscar was underneath it.

Next, he took them over to where the footprints had come up to the fallen tractor and stopped. Not surprisingly, they were gone, buried under the footprints of people who had come out to help the previous evening.

"So," Freddy said, "if you're saying it wasn't an accident, what are you saying? That Oscar committed suicide? Or that Oscar was murdered? That doesn't make any sense, either. Who would want to kill Oscar? I don't get it. It's got to have been an accident. That's the only explanation that makes sense."

Freddy and Cole both turned to look at the officers, waiting for a response

As they waited, Jake and Bob looked at each other, each waiting for the other to say something first.

For a while, there was a lot of waiting and not much talking going on. This was mostly because neither Bob nor Jake knew what to say. Until that moment, it had not even crossed their minds that what happened to Oscar could have been anything but an accident. Bob, in fact, had already finished the full draft of his accident report with blanks left to fill in with the information he was planning to collect from his morning visit to the bog.

When the silence became more awkward than he could handle, Bob broke it with a cough.

"Okay," he said, after clearing his throat two or three more times "it looks like I'm going to have to rewrite my incident report."

He paused and shot another look at Jake before turning back to Cole and asking, "Last night it didn't matter, but now it does. I've got to know for sure. Is Bog 6 on city or county land?"

Before Cole could answer, Jake added, "We're assuming that Oscar died in this bog. Who knows? Maybe he died, or was killed, somewhere else, but this is where we found him so which is it? City or county?"

"City," Cole answered. "Those bogs over to the east are county, but where we're standing is city."

As he spoke, Cole pulled a CD from his pocket and handed it to Bob.

"I put all the photos I took last night on this disk. You might want to take your own now that the light is better. Who knows, by tomorrow all the marks could be gone."

"Thanks, Cole," Jake replied. "It looks like we've got a lot of work to do."

"Let me know if you need anything," Cole said in reply. "I'll give you a free pass to do whatever you need to do in this bog. You can drive and walk around my property but don't step into any of the other bogs unless you check with me first. Now, if you'll excuse us, Freddy and I have a lot of work to do, too."

Cole turned and started walking back to his truck.

"C'mon, Freddy," he said over his shoulder. "Let's go someplace and talk."

"Fine with me, boss," Freddy answered." You know me; an unattached, single male with nothing but time on his hands. Your wish is my . . ."

"Shut up, Freddy," Cole shot back. "That's not the kind of talking I meant."

As they drove past Freddy's house to the main road, Cole pointed to the guesthouse.

"Oscar's truck is still there," he observed matter-of-factly. "I suppose the keys were in his pocket. I'll have to see if Marta has another set."

In one seamless motion, Cole stuck a Bluetooth into his ear, made a right turn onto the road and spoke the words, "Call Marta."

Two rings later, Marta answered the phone.

"Yes, I'm doing fine," she said. "Yes, the children are fine, too. Today they are staying home from school. We're all sad and don't know what to do. There are so many friends coming by already. I couldn't do this without Bel."

Cole asked a few more questions and Marta gave answers.

"Yes, I have a set of keys for the truck."

"No, I don't need the truck. Maybe tomorrow."

"Bel says she will be staying with me all day and again tonight if necessary. She is so nice. Thank you."

Cole couldn't figure out why Marta had said "Thank you" to him. As far as he could tell he hadn't done anything to earn it . . . at least not yet; but just to be polite he said, "You're welcome," anyway.

After grabbing two cups of coffee at the McDonald's drive-thru, Cole drove to the end of the Seaview beach access and parked the truck on the edge of the beach facing the ocean.

"What did you want to talk about," Freddy asked.

"I want to know what you did and what you saw yesterday. I want you to tell me everything you can remember."

Thirty minutes later, the coffee was gone and Freddy had run out of things to remember.

He had awakened at 6:00 a.m. He had eaten breakfast. He had driven across the river to Warrenton to pick up some parts for the new sprinkler system he was installing in Bog 12. When he got back, he drove over to Bog 12 to install the parts. On the way, he waved at Oscar who was just starting up the tractor in Bog 6. When he drove back to his house at 11:45 a.m. for lunch he noticed that Oscar and his truck were gone. When he left the house at 12:30 p.m., he noticed that Oscar's truck was once again parked in front of the guesthouse. He then drove towards town; mailed some packages at the Seaview Post Office; did some business at the bank; did some personal shopping at Sid's Market; and got back to the farm at 2:30 p.m. Oscar's car was still there, but he didn't notice where Oscar was or what he was doing at that point. This was because, instead of driving past Bog 6, he had gone the long way around the farm, past the McCrae's house. He had then stopped at Bog 16 on the farm's southeast corner, a bog that had not drained properly during the harvest. After clearing some debris, he returned to his house at 4:45. After noting that Oscar's truck was still parked in the same place, he went inside, fixed and ate dinner and was watching television at 6:30 p.m. when Cole called to tell him there had been an accident at Bog 6.

"Yes," Freddy said in response to Cole's questions. There were people in Warrenton who saw him there; and "Yes," he talked to people at the post office, the bank and at Sid's; and "No," he didn't see or talk to anyone from 2:30 p.m. until he received Cole's phone call at 6:30 p.m.

"Why do you want to know all of this?" he asked. "Let me guess: You want to know if I have an alibi. Do you think I killed Oscar?"

As he spoke, Freddy's face began to turn red and the pitch and volume of his voice began to rise.

"What's up with this?" he continued with a hint of anger edging into his voice. "I can see why the police might want to rake me over the coals, but you? I thought you trusted me more than that. Have I ever lied to you before? Have I ever cheated you? I've been clean and sober for five years and haven't taken drugs for over six. I even told you all about those things when you hired me. I have nothing to hide, so you might as well keep asking your stupid questions. I have answers . . ."

With those words, Freddy's voice trailed off into silence.

Cole sat in stunned silence, searching for words to calm Freddy down and reassure him that he was just trying to make sense out of what had happened to Oscar.

"Freddy, I'm not accusing you of anything," he said. "I trust you. You've been my right-hand man for four years. I just want to know how things played out yesterday. You were the one closest to the. . . "

Cole paused for a moment before working up the nerve to finish the sentence.

". . . closest to the scene of the crime. I'm sorry, Freddy. I still don't think it was an accident."

"Who would have wanted to kill Oscar?" Freddy shot back. "He didn't have an enemy in the world!"

"That's where we disagree," Cole replied. "I think he had at least one."

Freddy and Cole's eyes locked as Cole added, "That's all it takes; just one."

Cole's phone rang. It was Jake.

"We've done just about all we can do with the bog," Jake explained. "What we need to do now is move the tractor out of the way so we can get a clear look at what's underneath. We could call in a tow truck but it would have to drive into the bog and we don't want to cause more damage to it than necessary."

"So," Cole said, "why are you telling me this? I already gave you permission to tear up the bog if you needed to . . ."

"Here," Jake said, "I'll let you talk to Bob."

"Hey, Cole," Bob began, "we figured that if we had a rope or a cable that was long enough—and a winch--we could stretch it across Bog 7 from the north, hook it up to the tractor in Bog 6, block the wheels at the side, and pull it upright without damaging anything. We were just wondering if you had a rope or cable long enough . . . and a winch . . . do you have a winch? The roads between the bogs are pretty narrow . . . not wide enough for a car or truck to back up and get the tractor back on its feet."

"You know," Cole replied, "your idea might just work. Now that I think of it, we do have a few ropes long enough to reach that far. They might stretch out a bit while you're pulling but I think they'll hold up long enough to get the job done. Father used them for pulling things out of the bogs and for pulling the berries together during harvest. I'll get Freddy on it right away. He knows where they are and knows which of them would work best.

"And," he continued after remembering that Bob's question had two parts, "Freddy's truck has a winch on the front end. Here, hold on a sec while I ask Freddy."

"Don't bother," Freddy said. "I could hear the conversation from here. I'll try and find the ropes. I'm not so sure about the winch, though. It wasn't pulling very well the last time I used it and, with the harvest and everything, I haven't had time to work on it. If you want me to help, I'll do my best."

"That's all I ask," Cole replied with a smile, ". . . only your best!"

Thirty minutes later, back at the farm, Cole and Jake stood by as Freddy and Bob wrestled a large coil of heavy rope onto the back of Freddy's truck.

The rope proved long enough to reach across the Bog 7 to Bog 6 and strong enough not to snap as Freddy pulled the tractor back onto its wheels with the winch . . . which worked perfectly.

What they found under the tractor was, well . . . not very much.

"I could have sworn there was blood on the back of Oscar's head when he was pulled out from under the tractor last night," Bob noted. "But where his head was lying, there isn't any blood at all . . . at least not that I can see."

"I don't see any, either," Jake agreed, "but we should take some sand and vine samples just in case there's something on them we can't see. To be on the safe side, I suppose you ought to take a few pictures of the area before we dig it up."

While Bob took the pictures, Freddy excused himself and began the job of gathering the rope onto the back of his truck. Cole, however, wandered across the bog in the opposite direction, following the path he assumed the mysterious footprints had taken to and from the fallen tractor.

When he came to the south edge of the bog, he stepped up onto the dike that ran east-west through his bogs. To the east, he could see more bogs, including Bog 12, two bogs away, where Freddy had been replacing the sprinklers. To the south, he could see more bogs with his house in the distance. Close by to the west were the spots where the ambulance and his truck had parked the night before. Farther in the distance, he could see Freddy's house on the left and the guesthouse on the right. As he turned to look north, he found himself perfectly aligned with Jake and Bob, the now-erect tractor, the rope being winched back across Bog 7, and Freddy's truck on the parallel road on the far side of Bog 7.

"I'll be damned," he whispered to himself.

He pulled out his phone and began entering numbers to reach Don Milner at the mortuary.

Back in the bog, Jake was placing sand and vine samples into numbered evidence bags while Bob was fighting to stay awake.

"We'd better wrap this up soon," Bob yawned. "I've been on the job for over thirteen hours and I can hardly keep my eyes open."

"Just a few minutes more," Jake replied. "Unless the autopsy says something different, we're going to have to treat this like a crime scene. That means the yellow tape stays up and we post a guard until we've done everything we . . ."

Jake stopped talking and smiled to himself. As far as he could tell, Bob had fallen asleep standing up.

"Wake up, pal," he said as he put his hand on his partner's shoulder and gave it a little shake. "Time for you to go home and go to bed. You've got another night shift coming up this evening and I don't want you falling asleep on the job, especially if you're driving! If you're not too busy tonight, you can rewrite yesterday's incident report. I'll do the rest of it. Now git!"

"Thanks, Jake," Bob said with yet another yawn as he began walking towards the guesthouse where his patrol car was parked. "I'll download the pictures when I check in tonight."

Two minutes later, after stowing his samples in the gym bag where he kept his evidence-collecting gear, Jake began walking the same route to his own car.

As he walked, his thoughts ran as follows: *The police budget's so tight . . . I'm not sure I can afford to pay someone to guard the site for the next day or two . . . Can I afford* not, *to? . . . I'd better check with the county prosecutor and see what he thinks . . .*

Cole's thoughts, however, were running in a very different direction.

"Hello and good morning!"

The voice in his phone sounded cheerful . . . almost too cheerful for 9:25 a.m.

"This is Don Milner. What can I do for you?"

"G'morning, Don. This is Cole McCrae. Are you at the mortuary? There's something I need to know about Oscar's . . . the things that were in his pocket when you picked him up from here last night . . ."

"Sorry, Cole, I'm still at home, but maybe I can answer your question from here."

"When you went through Oscar's pockets before . . . before you did whatever you did with him last night . . . what did you find? I mean, is it all right for me to ask?"

"Uh, Cole, can you be a little more specific?"

"No, I don't think I can. I mean . . . did he have a wallet? Was there money in it? His truck keys? . . . That sort of thing."

"Why do you want to know?"

"Just curious, I guess. Maybe it's for Marta, so she knows where Oscar's things are."

"If Marta wants to know something she can call me herself."

There was a pause.

"Okay, Cole," Don continued, "I'll tell you this. There was a wallet. There was money, there was a comb . . . and that's about it."

"What?" Cole blurted. "There weren't any keys? Are you sure? He drove his truck here and then went out to work in the bogs. His truck is still parked in his usual spot."

Cole's brain was shifting gears like a semi-driver heading over Steven's Pass.

"I . . . I guess I'll have to get the spare truck keys from Marta," he stammered. "Uh, thanks. And, by the way, when will you get the autopsy report completed?"

"I've said enough," Don answered. "I'll be in touch with the police and with Marta, so if you have any more questions, you can ask them, okay? I'm sorry, but I've got to leave or I'll be late for an appointment."

There was another pause.

"Don't get me wrong," Don added, "I'm sorry about what happened to Oscar. As a matter of fact, I got to thinking about it last night after I went to bed—this might be the first fatality I've ever had related to cranberries . . ."

"Thanks, Don," Cole interrupted. "You've been more help than you know."

So, it wasn't about money, Cole thought to himself. *And I wasn't even thinking about Oscar's keys . . . What happened to the keys? He drove back here after lunch, parked his truck and . . . they have to be around here somewhere . . .*

He glanced up and saw Jake in the distance, walking with his back to him.

"Hey, Jake," he yelled. "Wait up!"

The Long Beach Police Chief put his evidence bag on the ground and turned around to see Cole trotting towards him.

What's he up to now? Jake sighed. *Ten to one he's already figured out who killed Oscar—"Colonel Mustard, in Bog 6, with the lead pipe . . ."*

Cole had hurried a bit too fast for his age and stood with his arms at his hips, sucking in as much oxygen as he could without hyperventilating.

"Well?" Jake asked, with an unintended inflection that betrayed his growing impatience.

"I've got an idea," Cole declared with breathless enthusiasm.

"Of course you do." Jake replied, with a hint of sarcasm in his voice. "What is it this time?"

"You need to get a metal detector; and the sooner the better."

"Why in God's name do I need a metal detector?" Jake stammered. "Wait, don't tell me—So I can find the murder weapon, right? Okay, since you've already got that figured out, why don't you just cut to the chase and tell me who killed Oscar and why? You can save me and the country prosecutor a whole lot of time and trouble if you'll just come out with it and stop beating around the bush. Don't mess with me, Cole. I've got a long day ahead of me . . ."

"No," Cole cut in, "It's not that. I have no idea what the murder weapon is . . . or if there even was a murder weapon . . . I mean there was a murder . . . but I'm just not sure whether there was a weapon or not . . ."

"Then what do I need a metal detector, for?" Jake shot back, trying hard to control his impatience.

"Oscar's keys are missing . . ."

". . .and," Jake cut him off, his voice now dripping with open sarcasm, "you promised Marta that the police department would be more than happy to find them for her. Sorry, Cole, if you want to find Oscar's keys, go ahead, be my guest; and while you're at it, you can be a Good Samaritan and pay it forward, or whatever else you want to do. I'd love to help but I'm already late for an appointment with Don Milner at the mortuary, followed by a conference call with the prosecutor's office . . ."

Jake's voice trailed off as he picked up his bag and began walking as fast as he could towards his car.

"Got to go," he shouted without turning his head. "Keep in touch . . . and keep those good ideas coming . . ."

I'm glad I'm not a cop, Cole mused as he watched Jake disappear into his patrol car. *I couldn't handle the stress.*

Instead of stressing, Cole pulled out his phone again and this time put in a call to his friend, Ruth, a recently remarried widow who Cole knew from church.

"Hello, this is Ruth," came the voice.

"Hello, Ruth, this is Cole McCrae. I need to borrow your metal detector."

"Why good morning, Mr. McCrae," Ruth replied. "I must say, you do come straight to the point. Let me think . . . my metal detector . . . Well, I suppose I've got some good news and some bad news for you. The bad news is that I gave my metal detector to one of my granddaughters as a Christmas present."

She paused for full dramatic effect before adding, "But the good news is that Ben bought me a new one to replace it and I'll be happy to loan it to you. When do you want me to bring it over? It's too high-tech for just anyone to use. It's taken me three weeks to get used to all the bells and whistles that came with it, so just point me in the right direction and I'll take it from there."

"That's a fair offer," Cole answered, "and I'll accept it right now if you're free. The only problem is that I don't what direction to point you in."

"That could complicate things a bit," Ruth countered. "What did you lose?"

"A needle in a haystack."

Part 3

With one hand, Cole turned off his phone and slipped it in his pocket. With his other hand, he waved down Freddy as his truck began a right turn in the direction of his house.

"Say, Freddy," Cole began after the truck had come to a full stop. "That rope looks awfully heavy. Do you need any help putting it away?"

"No," Freddy replied through the open driver's-side window. "I can manage. I've done it . . ."

Freddy paused before starting over, "It's okay. I'll figure something out, thanks."

As he started to drive off, Cole stopped him again by rapping his hand against the door.

"Freddy," Cole said, "This is a hard time for all of us. I'm going to take a few days off to think things over. Nothing has to be done that can't wait a few days. I want you to take the rest of the week off, too. If something needs to be done, I'll take care of it. Go home or leave town. It's all the same to me. Just be back in the saddle on Monday. Got it?"

"Got it, boss. But there are a few things I've got to finish up in Bog 12 . . ."

"I don't want to see you anywhere except 'at-ease.' Bog 12 will have to wait until next week."

Cole not only said the words but he stared them straight into Freddy's forehead.

Freddy gave a quick glance in the direction of Bog 12 before pressing his lips together and giving Cole a slight nod. As if to bring closure to the conversation, he rolled up the window and left Cole standing alone on the south side of Bog 6 waiting for Ruth to arrive with her metal detector.

Freddy's dust had hardly begun to settle when Cole's phone rang in his pocket. It was Bel.

147

"Cole, I've been talking to Marta and there's something I think you should know."

"Like, when you're coming home?"

"Yes, I suppose you should know that, too. Marta is going to drive me home later this afternoon, before dinner. We can eat out tonight if that's all right with you. But that's not why I called. I called because . . . . Is this a bad time to talk?"

"No, it's a good time. What were you going to tell me?"

"Marta has a nephew in Mexico who's gotten in with one of the drug cartels. She says this nephew called her and said he wanted Oscar to help him transport Mexican 'produce' from California to some markets in the Pacific Northwest.

"The first time he called, Oscar wouldn't even give a reply. He just told Marta to hang up on him. The second time the nephew called he hinted to Marta that someone closely related to her in Mexico might suffer an unfortunate accident if Oscar didn't agree to his offer. When Marta passed the message on to Oscar, he grabbed the phone and shouted obscenities in Spanish before hanging up. The third time the nephew called was two weeks ago. He said that if Oscar didn't agree to his offer then someone closely related to Marta in the Pacific Northwest would be the one to suffer an unfortunate accident. Oscar wasn't home at the time and when she asked her nephew who he was talking about he just laughed and said, 'Someone who's swimming in a tropical fish tank. Glub, glub,' and hung up."

"What's that supposed to mean?" Cole asked. "I mean the tropical fish thing?"

Bel was quick to reply, "An Oscar is a type of tropical fish that people sometimes have in their home aquarium. He must have been referring to Oscar, but neither Marta nor Oscar could figure out what the nephew was talking about. The nephew never called back and, since Oscar didn't have any way of contacting him, they just let the matter drop, thinking

148

that if they got another phone call they would talk to the police about it."

"So you think this might have something to do with what happened to Oscar yesterday? That someone from a Mexican cartel tipped a tractor on top of him because he wouldn't agree to be an ass? Or a mule? Or whatever they call it?"

"I think it's worth considering. After all, the coincidental timing couldn't have been much better . . . or worse . . . you know what I mean."

"Yeah, I know what you mean. But this is getting way too complicated for me. All I want to do is grow cranberries and make people happy."

"Cole? Has there been anyone hanging around from Mexico lately? I mean like someone who didn't belong here? Someone who might have come here to do something to Oscar?"

"No, I haven't noticed anyone like that . . . and I don't know a lot of people from around here who use drugs, either—like the kind from Mexico . . . the illegal drugs—or anyone who might be selling them . . ."

"What about the drug rehab programs on the Peninsula?" Bel suggested. "There's the one in Ocean Park and the one in Long Beach . . . maybe someone from one of those . . ."

"No," Cole cut in, "I don't think so. I doubt that drug cartels are slipping hit-men into drug rehab programs to give them cover so they can sneak out and assassinate people when nobody's looking."

"Cole," Bel said as her husband paused to take a breath, "I think Marta needs to go to the police and tell them what she told me. They need to start looking at what happened to Oscar as if it might be something more than an accident."

"I've already convinced them of that," Cole replied. "I also agree that Marta should share everything she knows with the police as soon as possible. Whoever did this to Oscar must have had a reason . . . a motive . . . and this Mexico drug connection is the first possible motive I've heard that makes any sense."

After taking a moment to think it over, Bel decided, "I'll talk to Marta about it and if she agrees, I'll get her over to the police station after lunch, before she drives me home."

"Good," Cole said, "and then we can go out for dinner! I love you, Bel. You're a good woman and a good wife. I'll see you later this afternoon. Bye."

While he was talking to Bel, Cole had walked over to where Freddy had parked the farm truck in front of the guesthouse next to Oscar's pickup. As Cole said the word, "Bye," Freddy came out of his house across the way carrying a small duffle bag. After opening the door to his garage and tossing the bag into the cab of his own pickup, he backed out and sped onto the main road so quickly he almost collided with Ruth's subcompact as she pulled in looking for Cole.

"G'morning, Ruth," Cole greeted as she stepped out of the car. "Welcome to the opening day of hunting season."

"I'm afraid I don't have a license," Ruth shot back. "If I had known what I was going to be hunting for I would have picked one up on my way over. I suppose it has something to do with the man who was killed here yesterday. Ben told me about the accident after you phoned. I'm so sorry. I can't imagine . . ."

"It's been hard on all of us. Oscar had a wife and two children. Bel's still at their house trying to help out. But that's what I need you for, too . . . to help me with something. After we found Oscar, we noticed his keys were missing. They weren't in his pockets and they should have been since he had just driven here in his truck."

Cole pointed to Oscar's pickup.

"Maybe he left the keys in the truck," Ruth suggested.

Cole slapped himself on the forehead.

"I never thought of that. It's so obvious. That's got to be where they are. Let's take a look."

The truck was unlocked but after searching through every possible hiding place and not finding anything but old gasoline receipts and loose change, Cole looked at Ruth, shrugged his shoulders in resignation, and closed the door on his side of the pickup.

"Good ideas are not always successful ones," Ruth said as she closed the door on her side. "Now what?"

"Let's see if you can find the keys in Bog 6. If you don't mind driving we can save a few steps."

"Sure," Ruth replied as she got into her car. "Hop on in and away we go."

A moment later as they got out of the car Ruth asked the obvious question.

"What about the yellow tape? It says, 'Do not cross.'"

"I completely forgot about that," Cole said. "I've been ignoring it ever since they put it up so I suppose we can ignore it now. In any case, Chief Jake told me I could look for the keys so I assume that included permission to look in the bog. Let's start in the corner next to the tractor. That's where the . . . that's where we found Oscar."

Ruth worked the metal detector like a pro and it didn't take long before they concluded that the keys weren't in Bog 6. They then systematically swept the ground along every possible route that Oscar could have taken to or from his truck. Once again, they found nothing.

"Where else could he have been?" Ruth asked. "Was there anyone else around that he might have talked to, or something he needed to get for the tractor or the mower, like a wrench or something?"

"The closest tools are in the shed next to the guest house and we've already checked that area. The only other person out here yesterday was Freddy. He told me he spent the

151

morning working in Bog 12, but he spent the afternoon working over in the southeast corner of the property. That would have been a long way for Oscar to walk."

"Maybe Freddy stopped by Bog 12 on his way to the other place," Ruth offered, "and maybe Oscar walked over to talk with him there. . ."

"No," Cole responded, "Freddy specifically said that he didn't drive that way, he went around the property past my house."

"I don't know much about your farm except for the places we've been this morning," Ruth mused. "But the only other place you've mentioned that is nearby and has anything to do with yesterday is Bog 12. When I go treasure hunting, I follow hunches all the time. I say we either check out Bog 12 or call it quits for the day. It's past Noon already and I'm getting hungry."

"You know," Cole said, "that might be worth a try. The police and I already agree that Oscar might have been killed somewhere else. There should have been blood on the ground where we found his body and there wasn't any. And I still don't see how the tractor could have fallen over on him the way it did if he had been alive at the time . . ."

"What?" Ruth gasped, "Are you saying this wasn't an accident? That Oscar might have been murdered and his body moved to Bog 6 after he was already dead?"

"That's one way to look at it," said Cole.

"Then maybe he lost his keys where he was killed . And who was around here that might have killed him? You mentioned Freddy; was there anyone else?"

Cole's phone rang again. It was Chief Jake.

"Have you found the keys yet?" he began without bothering to say "Hello." "If you do, don't touch them. They might be evidence. Hey, look, I'm sorry the way I behaved a while ago. I was running late and I guess I just lost my cool. I talked with Don and he mentioned that you asked him about the keys. That's when it all began to make sense that the keys might have something to do with the case. Then I talked to the prosecutor and he said to leave the tape up but not to worry about a guard, and now Marta's coming by in a few minutes to tell me something about Mexican drug cartels. Bob's at home sleeping off a long night and the other day-officers are tied up with presentations at the elementary schools. I'm glad to have you help out any way you can. If I could, I'd appoint you a temporary deputy or something. Let me know if you find anything or if you come up with another one of those ideas."

"It's all good, Jake," Cole replied when he heard the Chief pause to take a breath, "I haven't found the keys yet, but I'm still looking. I'll be interested to hear what you think about what Marta's going to tell you."

"What?" Jake sighed. "You already know about that, too? Oh, of course, you do. Bel's been helping out on that end, hasn't she? Thanks, Cole. Keep in touch."

Cole stuffed the phone back in his pocket and reached out both hands towards Ruth.

"Here let me carry that for you. It's the least I can do."

"Take it," Ruth said, handing him the detector, "and thank you for giving me a call. I love looking for things and if I can help solve whatever it was that happened to Oscar then that would be icing on the cake for me."

Two minutes later, they were standing at the northwest corner of Bog 12. Because the sprinklers needed to be replaced, it had been the first bog Oscar pruned after the harvest. Most of the new sprinkler system was already installed with the exception of the middle area next to the road where a small assortment of metal pipes and sprinkler heads lay scattered on the sand.

153

"We might as well start there," Cole said, pointing to the place.

Ruth stepped into the bog and turned on the detector.

"No need to walk the same area twice," she said. "I'll start here and work my way over. When I'm finished with that area I'll run the same pattern I used at Bog 6 to . . ."

Ruth stopped talking in mid-sentence as the metal detector emitted a soft, high-pitched whine.

"That didn't take very long," she joked as she bent over to brush away some sand in the middle of what was clearly someone's footprint.

"Well, I'll be . . ." she whispered to herself, but loudly enough for Cole to hear.

"What did you find?" Cole asked eagerly.

"You said that if I found the keys I wasn't supposed to touch them, right?"

"That's right. That's what I said . . . Why?"

"Well, I'm not touching them, because there they are," she explained as she pointed to the ground.

Cole reached into his pocket, pulled out his phone and called Chief Jake.

"What now, Cole," came the Chief's voice. "If you've come up with another idea could you put it on hold for a few minutes? I'm trying to finish my notes from what Marta just told me."

"We found Oscar's keys."

"Oh!" Jake spoke with some enthusiasm. "Where were they?"

"In Bog 12, where Freddy was working yesterday morning."

"Hmm," Jake hmmed, "As far as I can tell, you and Freddy are my only suspects in this case. Unless, of course, Marta killed Oscar during lunch, drove him over to your place in his pickup, carried his body into Bog 6, took the keys out of his pocket and threw them the length of a football field into Bog 12, pushed the tractor onto his body and then walked home to make it look as if he drove the truck there himself."

"Uh, Chief . . ." Cole interrupted.

"Speaking of Freddy," Jake continued, "I need to sit down and interview him about yesterday."

"It'll have to wait until Monday," Cole interrupted again. "I told him to take the rest of the week off. He threw a bag into his truck and drove off almost three hours ago. . ."

"You *what*?" Jake shouted, his enthusiasm suddenly replaced by utter disbelief. "Let me get this straight: Someone may have been murdered and you order the main suspect to leave town? Are you nuts?"

"It's okay, Chief," Cole said as soothingly as possible. "He's got a cell phone. I'll just call him and tell him that his vacation's been cancelled."

"Sure, Cole," came the reply. "He'll make a u-turn at the Mexican border just so he can drive back and be interrogated as a suspect in a murder case."

"I just wanted him out of the way so I could . . . so *we* could search the bogs and gather evidence without him . . . being in the way . . . I guess I blew it . . . sorry, Jake. I don't know what got into me."

"What's done is done," Jake sighed. "Who knows, he might turn out to be as innocent as Marta, and maybe your phone call will bring him back like a homing pigeon."

There was a long pause that lasted until Jake broke it with, "So you found the keys . . ."

More silence.

"Cole," Jake continued. "Don't go telling anyone but I think I'm in over my head on this one. Don't touch the keys. Don't touch anything. Don't take another step into a bog . . . any bog. Go home and stay there, or go somewhere, but stay away from the crime scene until I'm done doing what I need to do. I'm going to call in the forensics team from the State Patrol. If this isn't done right, some judge is going to overthrow a conviction on a stupid technicality and some rat-faced murderer will walk free instead of going to jail where he or she belongs. I'm going to put out an APB on Freddy. I want him back here pronto whether you get him on the phone or not."

The Chief felt like ending the call by slamming the phone's handset onto the phone cradle. But cell phones don't offer the same satisfaction as rotaries, so he had to be content with poking the "End Call" button as hard as he could without sending the phone clear across the room.

That more or less wraps up this story . . . except for mentioning that later that evening Cole and Bel went over to the Drop Anchor Restaurant and ordered French Dip sandwiches for dinner.

It might also be worth mentioning that the autopsy showed Oscar died instantly from a blow to the back of his neck with an object the size and shape of a two-inch diameter metal irrigation pipe. The forensics report found DNA traces of blood and skin on the tip end of Oscar's truck key that matched Freddy's DNA exactly. Forensics also found traces of Oscar's blood in the sand adjacent to the pile of irrigation pipe in Bog 12. The following morning, the California Highway Patrol picked up Freddy just south of Redding. On his left forearm were fresh needle marks, and a deep scrape consistent with being stabbed by the point of a key. On his phone was a number that was later matched with one known to have been used by Marta's nephew.

At the trial, Cole testified that it was his opinion that if Freddy could pull a tractor upright by using a rope and a truck winch, he could have used the same method to pull the tractor over on top of Oscar's body. Freddy pleaded innocent by virtue of self-defense, claiming that Oscar attacked him after he refused to team up with Oscar to transport drugs from California to Seattle. In the end, the jury saw it the other way around and found Freddy guilty of second-degree murder. The judge did not discover any technicalities that required him to overrule the conviction.

Bel baked a fresh batch of brownies for Oscar's funeral.

The uneaten brownies she had baked for Cole were frozen, and later shared at church during an after-worship fellowship time. Ruth said they tasted delicious.

There were no brownies for Freddy.

On the Wings of the Wind

She was twenty-one . . . He was twenty-seven.

She was from Raymond, Washington . . . He was from somewhere else.

She had been sexually abused as a child . . . He had been easily amused as a child.

At sixteen, she had run away from home . . . At eighteen, he had enlisted in the Army.

She had gone to Seattle . . . He had gone everywhere.

She had been beaten by boyfriends . . . He had been wounded in Iraq.

She was single, unattached, and alone . . . He was single, unattached, and alone.

She was standing at the edge of the Pacific Ocean in Long Beach, Washington, with no money, no place to go, and no reason to live . . . He was standing at the edge of the Pacific Ocean in Long Beach, Washington, flying a kite.

"Incoming! Head's up! Duck or get out of the way!"

The young woman did not respond, apparently oblivious or indifferent to both the shouted warning and the untethered kite that dropped out of the sky and fluttered onto the sand four feet to her left.

"Close call."

The voice was a man's voice. The woman heard it and could tell it was coming closer.

"I'm sorry if I frightened you."

The woman was facing the ocean and the man was talking to her back. Above her flip-flops, he could see random fragments of her legs peeking through holes in a pair of frayed and faded blue jeans. A long gray and brown serape covered whatever she was wearing above her waist, and her long, tangled blonde hair was held in check by a forward-facing baseball cap.

As he bent to pick up the kite, he caught a glimpse of her profile, noting her lips were pressed tightly together, her eyes were closed, and her arms were folded over her chest. It crossed his mind that if she had been lying down, she would have looked like a corpse.

"Excuse me, Ma'am," he said, with the ingrained formality drilled into those who have served in the military, "are you all right?"

She turned on him with the speed of a rattlesnake that has patiently lured its prey to within striking distance.

"Don't 'Ma'am' me!" she hissed. "I ain't your Mama. Go to hell and leave me alone."

"Nice to meet you, too," he replied with a smile as he straightened up with the kite in his hand. "My name is Derek."

"Like I said, 'Go to hell and . . .'"

"' . . . and leave me alone.'" He interrupted, finishing the sentence.

The intended effect of her glare was lost as she found herself bending her head back and staring straight into the sun. Derek, she discovered, was six inches taller than she was.

"You're not making a very good first impression," he continued as he stepped away from the sun and stood facing her with his back to the ocean.

"Go to hell and . . ."

" . . . and leave me alone," he interrupted for the second time, "not to mention that you could use a new scriptwriter. You're repeating yourself."

She opened her mouth to curse him again but hesitated, leaving the unspoken expletive dissolving under her tongue like a tab of acid.

She could see him clearly now. He was barefoot, wearing blue board shorts and a t-shirt that featured the image of a large, hexagonal kite and the words, "Long Beach, Washington, International Kite Festival." He had shaved his head, but a receding hairline was clearly visible, betrayed by a three-day growth of hair on both his head and his face. His eyes were blue, his skin tanned, and his facial expression made him look like someone who had just heard a joke and was about to explode into laughter.

She closed her mouth and returned his smile with a sneer.

For some unknown reason Derek felt drawn to her. He searched her face with an intensity that bordered on intimacy and noted her eyes were blue like his own. Her left cheek was marred by a fading bruise and, where her right eye met the ridge of her nose, there was a small, delicate tattoo of a single tear.

"Well, it looks like I'm done for the day," he said cheerily. "How about a cup of coffee?"

The question was not asked in a vacuum. Above their heads, a hundred kites turned the cloudless sky into a sun-shifting kaleidoscope of shapes and colors, while around them, hundreds of men, women and children stood watching as the mid-morning kite fighting competition narrowed to the final two contestants. It was August, and the annual kite festival was in full swing.

As far as the woman was concerned, her surroundings were at best irrelevant or at worst annoying. Her early morning walk down the Bolstad Avenue beach access had taken her past dozens of festival food and clothing vendors. The street, by dead-ending on the beach, became an apt metaphor for her life. By the time she stepped off the pavement, her life had literally, as well as figuratively, come to the end of the road. It was a fact as hard as the packed sand under her feet and as cold as the treacherous stretch of ocean in front of her.

For over two hours, she had been standing in that spot trying to decide what to do. Short of throwing herself into the water, she had not come up with a single idea that appealed to her. She had spent her last dollar the night before on a small-sized serving of McDonald's fries. As she ate the fries, she recalled the story of a man condemned to die who had been offered the choice of anything he wanted for his final dinner. He had chosen a McDonald's Happy Meal. The irony in the recollection was hard to miss.

She ate the fries as slowly as possible, savoring the shelter of the restaurant until the place closed at 11:00 p.m. The midsummer evening was warm and dry so she chose to spend the night under a tree on the edge of the dunes just south of the public restrooms at the Sid Snyder beach access. It was not the first time she had slept outdoors, but before the sun came up that morning she made up her mind it was never going to happen again.

Now, standing on the beach, she had run out of ideas.

God! she groaned, *Throw me a rope Make something happen. Help me, O Lord, for the waters have come up to my neck!*

The last phrase caught her up short. It had popped into her head from nowhere. It sounded familiar, like something she might have read in the Bible back when her father had still been alive—back when he had read devotions at breakfast each morning—back when she had been dropped off for Sunday school once or twice each month—back before her mother had remarried—back then—before history—before time began—before the darkness had descended on her like a shroud.

"Incoming!"

The word awakened her as if from a dream.

"Head's up! Duck . . .!"

She immediately resented the interruption. She had known too many men and this one was not going to be any different. As far as she was concerned they were all alike. Even so, without a place to live she had been desperate enough to allow them to use and abuse her as they liked. She had been treated like trash so often she had come to believe it was what she was: Trash—worthless, useless, unwanted garbage.

"Go to hell!" she screamed. It was as if her subconscious had intervened in a final, desperate attempt to assert herself as a human being—as if spitting in this man's face might somehow cleanse, redeem, and empower her to declare to the world: "I am Vanessa! I am *somebody!*"

"How about a cup of coffee?"

She was fighting for her life, but Vanessa was, if nothing else, a survivor. She had asked God to throw her a rope and she was both shrewd enough to spot it and desperate enough to take it when it was offered to her.

Coffee sounds good, she said to herself as she manipulated her sneer into a semi-sweet imitation of a smile, *and maybe I can milk this guy for something more.*

163

She shifted gears from "assertive" to "passive" in a blink of an eye, suddenly willing to trade both body and soul for food and a bed . . . even for one night . . .

His steady gaze made her feel weak and uncomfortable. It had been a long time since she had worked up the courage to look any man straight in the eye. Now she had tried it and had been the first to blink.

She lowered her eyes and managed to squeeze out the words, "A cup of coffee? . . . Sure . . . Just don't call me, 'Ma'am,' okay?"

"Deal," he said. "But I've got to call you something. Do you have a name?"

"Vanessa," she said softly as she turned and began retracing her steps back towards town.

"Hold on, Vanessa" he said. "I've got to dismantle the kite and pack it up first."

She stood with her back to him, staring at the ocean until he was done.

They walked more or less side by side but without saying anything to each other until they passed under the place where the words, "The World's Longest Beach," are famously inscribed on the Long Beach Arch.

"My car's over there," Derek said, pointing to a crowded, temporary parking area on their left. "I'll stash the kite in the trunk."

As they approached the car, Vanessa asked, "What's with the kite? Are you one of those . . . uh . . . kite flying people?"

"I'll tell you all about it when we sit down. Where do you want to go? Scoopers for an ice cream? Cottage Bakery for coffee?"

"Do they have food there? Like a sandwich or something? I missed breakfast."

"Sure, whatever you want. It's on me, remember?"

As they sat facing each other across a table at the bakery, Vanessa tried hard not to inhale her ham and cheese sandwich in one bite.

I've got to play this right, she thought. *So . . . slow . . . down, Vanessa. This sucker might be the only chance you're going to get.*

She took a small sip from her large Mountain Dew and watched as Derek attacked his Devil Dog pastry with a plastic knife and fork.

"So?" she asked, trying hard to hide her complete disinterest in the subject. "The kite? Tell me about the kite."

"It's not all that interesting," he began, to which Vanessa replied by nodding her head in total agreement. "But since you asked . . ."—he paused for a sip of coffee—"After I recovered from my first deployment to Iraq, I was given a short, non-combat assignment in Kabul . . ."

"Iraq? Kabul?" Vanessa interrupted. "You were in the army or something?"

"Yeah—for seven years," he explained. "Twice to Iraq and once to Afghanistan . . . Kabul . . . It was in the middle of winter. I don't think the temperature went above zero the whole time I was there."

He paused to take another sip of coffee.

"Anyway, they showed us a movie in Kabul—it had just been released—the troops get new movies when they come out—for morale, I guess. *The Kite Runner*: that was the name of the movie. It was about a boy who lived in Afghanistan back in the 1970s and '80s when Russia was trying to run the country. I guess the important thing is that he got involved in flying a kite—kite fighting—where two or more people try to cut each other's kites down while they're in the air—I mean while their *kites* are in the air, not the people . . ."

I must sound like an ass, he groaned to himself as he took a bite of pastry and another sip of coffee.

165

"Well," he continued, "the kite thing looked like fun, so a couple of the other guys and I got together and made kites out of some coat hangers, newspaper, tape, and string, and tied on some rags for a tail. After some trial and error, we ended up building some pretty good kites. It passed the time, even though the wind chill left our faces numb from the cold.

"When I got out two years ago I took a class on how to build and fly kites. There are so many different kinds of kites—that's what the kite festival is all about—to show off all the different kinds of kites."

Vanessa was trying to keep her boredom under control by alternating bites from her sandwich with sips of soda. The boredom was winning.

"Oh," Derek said as a new thought came into his head, "did you know there's a kite museum here in town? It's awesome!"

Derek's enthusiasm quickly faded as he noticed that Vanessa's eyes were beginning to look as glazed as a pair of donut holes. Only half of this was from boredom, of course. The other half was because she hadn't had a decent night's sleep in a bed for three days.

"So . . ." he said hurriedly, trying to get the story over as quickly as possible, "I got involved in kite fighting as a hobby and that's what I was doing on the beach when I almost dropped my kite on your head."

As he spoke the final word, Vanessa's eyes closed and her head settled onto the table. The caffeine in the Mountain Dew had not been enough to keep her awake.

Derek sighed, gave a small shrug and tried hard not to laugh out loud.

Atta boy, Derek, you really know how to impress a girl!

He stared intently at Vanessa's face as he finished his Devil Dog and coffee. Several strands of hair had escaped the confines of her cap and were lying loosely across the upturned side of her face.

She looks so peaceful, he decided. *She's even prettier when she's asleep.*

He got up from the table and asked the server to bring a take-out container for what was left of Vanessa's sandwich.

"Psst!" he said quietly into her ear. "Wake up! It's time to go!"

"Go where?" she mumbled, only half awake. "There's nowhere to go . . . no . . . where . . . to . . . go . . ."

Derek shook her gently until her eyes opened. When she saw him looming over her, she threw her hands up in front of her face and said in a voice loud enough for everyone in the bakery to hear, "Who are you?" Then adding, as she looked around the room, "Where am I? What are you doing? Get away from me!"

Her head cleared enough to remember that her questions had answers.

"Uh, you're Derek, right?" she asked in a softer, calmer voice.

"Yes," he said, as he sat down next to her. "And you're Vanessa.

"Say," he continued, "you look like you could use a nap. Where are you staying? I'll walk there with you or, if it's too far to walk, I'll drive, okay?"

Here's my chance, she thought, suddenly feeling wide awake.

"I don't have a place yet," she said, *ad libbing* like a stand-up comedian at the Improv, "but I would sure like to lie down for a while. Maybe I could crash at your place . . . if that's all right with you?"

"Sure, why not. I'm just a block away, but I need to get my car. We can drive."

167

He paused, trying to think. *There's something I'm forgetting.*

"Oh," he said, "do you have a suitcase? Or a backpack or something . . . you know . . . with your clothes and things?"

"Over there," she said, pointing through the bakery door at the store across the street. "I left it when they opened this morning. It's behind the counter."

They crossed the street, grabbed the small backpack, walked to the car, drove two blocks to the motel, parked the car, walked past the front desk and up a flight of stairs to a room on the second floor.

"Pretty lucky, I guess," Derek said as they stepped through the door. "I asked for a King but all they had left was a room with two Queens. This one's mine," he said, pointing to the one closest to the bathroom. "You can have that one."

The pause that followed was awkward, at least for Derek.

"Don't, uh, worry about me. . . uh . . . the beds are 'His' and 'Hers' and I promise I won't get them mixed up. If you want, I'll see if they have another room available . . . I mean if you want privacy . . . otherwise, I'm okay with sharing . . . or I'll sleep in the lobby . . ."

Vanessa's brain was racing through her options. On the one hand, he was offering her a private room . . . it couldn't get any better than that . . . but . . .the only way she knew how to say "thank you" was to maybe do some snuggling, and that would mean sharing the room, and probably one of the two beds. He seemed like a nice guy . . . nicer than any of the boyfriends she had lived with the past few years. Maybe he would even be nice to her . . . sweet to her . . . and gentle . . .

Shut yourself up, girl! she told herself. *He's a guy. Don't trust him. Take the separate room. Just for once, do yourself a favor!*

On the other hand, she continued, *I might get more than one night out of this if I do a little snuggling . . . Besides, a girl's got to eat.*

"That's nice of you," she heard herself say, "but if it's all right, I'll just lie down here for now. I really could use a nap. I didn't sleep well last night."

She glanced around the room and saw her reflection in a mirror.

It had been a long time since she had seen herself in a mirror . . . not counting the ones in public restrooms. The woman she saw staring back looked frayed around the edges, like the pants she was wearing—worn and dirty. The woman in the mirror appeared gaunt and thin, reminding her of a high school friend named Claire, who had been bulimic but kept it a secret from everyone until she told Vanessa and made her promise not to say anything to anyone.

There was a time when Vanessa had taken pride in how she looked. Her hair, her nails, her skin, her makeup, they all made her feel special when she looked her best. But her last two boyfriends had convinced her she was trash and, over time, she had begun to look the part. Not that it mattered. The last boyfriend was usually too drunk or too stoned to notice or care what she looked like as long as she did what he wanted.

But now, with Derek in the room she felt dirty . . . dirty like a whore . . . and, worse than that, she smelled! She couldn't remember the last time she had felt so ashamed and embarrassed about the way she looked and about the person she had become.

She grabbed her pack and headed straight for the bathroom.

"I need a shower," she said brusquely, as she slammed and locked the door behind her.

Derek kicked back on his bed and turned on the television. He found nothing of interest and turned it off. The sound of the shower reminded him that there was an attractive young woman *sans* clothes just a few feet from where he was lying. The thought stirred his body in a pleasant way and he allowed himself to indulge his fantasy even as the sound of running water transitioned into the whirring of a blow dryer.

To his surprise, the woman who emerged from the bathroom did not look much different from the one who had gone in. She wore the same pair of torn jeans and the same faded Guns N' Roses t-shirt she had been wearing under her serape. Her still-damp hair hung heavily over her shoulders and down her back, looking as if she had tried to smooth it without the benefit of a brush. He wondered if she had changed her underwear.

That final thought curbed his stirrings like a bucket of ice water poured into his lap.

"Hey," she said, as she walked across the room and lay down on her bed.

"Hey," he replied as he watched her curl up into a fetal position with her back to him.

She was asleep within seconds.

It was 11:55 a.m. when she fell asleep and 4:20 p.m. when she woke up.

Derek spent the afternoon lying on his bed watching her sleep—wondering what sort of a mess he had gotten himself into and trying to figure out what he was going to do next. At the bakery, he had reached the conclusion that Vanessa was broke, homeless, and probably willing to steal his wallet if she thought she could get away with it.

Part of him felt sorry for her, casting himself in the role of a Good Samaritan tending to the wounds of someone he had found beaten and bleeding along the side of a road.

Another part of him felt attracted to her—not in a sexual way (his shower fantasy not withstanding), or even in a romantic way. Beneath her obvious sadness—beneath the armor plate that she wore to protect her broken spirit—he sensed there was beauty waiting to be set free.

The thought reminded him of something his mother had warned him about when he was in the sixth grade.

"Derek," she said, "you've got a good heart, but you've got to accept people for the way they are. You can't go around trying to 'fix' them or to reshape them into something you want them to be. Only God can do that, and you are definitely *not* God!"

To make the point she went to the library and checked out the movie, *My Fair Lady.*

"Watch it," she told him, "and then we'll talk."

Derek never forgot the conversation that followed.

"Don't be Professor Higgins," his mother said. "Don't try to turn every Eliza Doolittle into someone they're not. You can love them, you can help them, you can be friends with them, but you've got to let them choose who they want to be. Treat them like people and not like some sort of personal home improvement project."

Even as a child he had been attracted to people who didn't seem fit in: the kids at school who couldn't speak English, the old people at church who sat by themselves during worship, people who looked sad or depressed like Vanessa.

Damn, he muttered.

Now he'd gone and done it again, offering to share his motel room with a girl he had just met on the beach because he felt sorry for her.

One night . . . just one night . . . and then she'll be gone, he promised himself, knowing full well that he was already looking forward to taking her out to dinner.

171

He closed his eyes, rested his head on a pillow and drifted into unconsciousness.

"Hey, Derek!"

The tropical beach and the friendly blonde girl who had been sunning herself next to him dissolved into consciousness.

When he opened his eyes, he was surprised to find that the friendly blonde girl had reappeared and was now bending over him in a motel room.

"You were snoring," she said. "It woke me up, but that's okay, I needed to get up."

"Snoring?" he yawned. "Oh . . . sorry about that. Sometimes I snore so loud it wakes *me* up! I must have fallen asleep. What time is it?"

She glanced at the bed stand clock.

"4:25," she said.

"Afternoon or morning?"

"I can't tell, the curtains are closed."

This time it was Vanessa who had been staring intently at Derek. She hadn't intended her comment about the curtain as a joke, but she could tell from the smile on his face that Derek thought it was funny.

She took a step backwards as he swung his feet over the side of the bed, stood up, and stretched his arms into the air until his hands nearly touched the ceiling.

"I need some air," he announced as he bent over and placed the palms of his hands flat on the floor without bending his knees. "Let's go for a walk."

He stood up, glanced across the room at the closed curtains and shot a wink in her direction.

"I'll just assume it's afternoon . . ."

As he slipped on a pair of sandals, Vanessa dangled one of her flip-flops in front of his face. The thong part had pulled out from the sole.

"Looks like they finally wore out," she said matter-of-factly. "They're the only shoes I've got."

Derek took a quick personal inventory.

Let's see . . . lunch . . . a bed in a motel . . . dinner coming up. . . and now a new pair of slippers . . . At this rate she'll have me buying her a car before breakfast. Maybe it's a good thing I fell asleep with my wallet in my back pocket instead of on the bed stand . . .

After checking to make sure the wallet was still intact, he said, "There's a store next door. If you can walk that far I'll buy you a new pair."

Fifteen minutes and a $50 pair of sandals later, they were on Sid Snyder Drive walking towards the beach.

"That's the kite museum," Derek said, pointing across the street. "They close in ten minutes but we can check out the gift store for free, if you want. They've got posters from all the kite festivals and a collection of photos of all the personalized license plates that kite fliers have on their cars."

Vanessa suddenly felt as if she was back at the Cottage Bakery fighting another losing battle with boredom.

What is it about kites that makes me want to throw up? She wondered.

Just a block in front of them, a myriad of kites hovered over the beach looking as if a flock of origami cranes had suddenly come to life. The effect was stunning.

Maybe it's not the kites, she continued wondering, *maybe it's the people who fly them . . . people like Derek. They all look so happy and smug—as if they don't have anything better to do or anything to worry about except flying kites and going home to big houses and fancy cars with personalized license plates.*

She stopped walking and stood with her fists clenched, waiting until Derek stopped and turn around.

"Why'd you stop?" he asked. "Is it the museum . . . ?"

"Damn you, Derek!" she suddenly screamed. "Damn you! Damn your mother! You're full of . . ."

Derek was disappointed but not surprised by the outburst. He had already seen her anger on the beach that morning and caught another glimpse of it when she slammed the bathroom door in their motel room. From what he had already guessed about her situation, he figured she probably had reasons to be angry. He didn't take her cursing personally because he didn't think it really had much to do about him at all. If anything, he was more embarrassed for her than for himself.

After a short time the cursing and swearing simmered down to a whisper and, when the whisper turned to silence, Vanessa sank to the ground sobbing softly.

Derek dropped to his knees and reached out to comfort her with a hug.

"Go to hell and leave me alone!" she shouted as she began beating him back with her fists.

The blows knocked him off balance and he found himself tipping over backwards onto the sidewalk, laughing.

"Like I said," he shouted up at the sky, "You need to find a new scriptwriter!"

Derek's response to her outburst confused her. She had expected him to retaliate with a slap to her face, a punch to her jaw or a kick to her stomach. The one thing she hadn't expected was laughter.

Was he mocking her? Was the laughter his way of showing contempt? or maybe he wasn't man enough defend himself against a girl . . .

She pictured him in full combat gear, with M-16 in hand, cowering on the ground in fear of her tiny fists. But that was the wrong image. He wasn't lying on the ground cowering at all. He was lying on the ground laughing. He had shown her nothing but kindness since the moment they met and she had done everything possible to take advantage of him. For the second time that day, she felt ashamed in his presence. She was trash, but he didn't treat her like trash. If he knew what she was really like she figured he would kick her aside like an empty beer can.

"Excuse me?"

Vanessa looked up and saw a middle-aged man standing a few feet away.

"Do you need any help?" he asked. "Would you like me to call the police?"

She turned to look at Derek and saw that he was now sitting up with an enormous smile on his face and a smear of something that looked like blood on his upper lip. She looked at her feet and saw the new pair of sandals. She looked towards the ocean and saw the kites being hauled down for the night. She looked around and saw men, women and children on both sides of the street walking towards town after enjoying an afternoon on the beach.

Her confusion was paralyzing. She couldn't decide whether to cry, to curse or to laugh.

After sneaking a second glance at Derek, she turned her head back towards the man and took a deep breath.

"No," she said, simply, "I don't need any help. I'm fine . . . really . . . I'm fine . . .and don't call the police, okay? . . . I'm fine . . ."

Derek stood and reached out his hand to help her up, but she wouldn't take it, preferring to stand up on her own. Without a word, they continued their walk towards the beach as if nothing had happened.

As they walked, Vanessa's eyes fixed themselves on Derek's face. He was sucking his upper lip, which was already beginning to swell. Instead of a smile, his face had taken on a more serious expression, as if he was deep in thought.

Vanessa was doing some serious thinking herself as she tried to sort out why she had exploded in rage and why she had started crying.

The anger part was easy to figure out—she hated everybody. She hated the world and everything in it. She especially hated happy, smiling people who had money, and families, and who flew kites on the beach while she had nothing except nightmare memories she couldn't forget and five years of regrets she couldn't forgive herself for.

The crying part was harder to explain.

As they passed the public restrooms, Vanessa stopped walking and stood staring at the line of trees where she had spent the previous night. Derek stopped, too, but this time he kept his distance as if unsure whether Vanessa was going to start swearing at him again.

Why, he wondered, *is she staring at the bathrooms?*

This time, however, he kept the question to himself and simply stood quietly waiting until Vanessa redirected her gaze at him and resumed walking towards the beach.

After only a few steps, she stopped again, lowered her head, stared straight down at the sidewalk, and waited until she had Derek's full attention.

"It's not you," she said quietly, "it's me. I'm the one who's all screwed up. You're nice . . . and kind . . ."

She lifted her head and looked directly into his eyes. Derek watched as a single tear formed in the corner of her right eye and paused next to its tattooed twin before sliding down her cheek and dropping to the ground.

When they began walking again he had the distinct feeling she had moved an inch or two closer to him than she had been before.

As they neared the beach, he steered her to the right, up a wooden ramp.

"Let's go on the Boardwalk," he said. "It will take us up to Bolstad where we were this morning. It's the easiest way to walk on the beach without getting sand between your toes."

Vanessa continued to stare at Derek as they walked, wondering what he was thinking.

What Derek was thinking was the same thing he had been thinking back in the motel room—he was thinking that hooking up with Vanessa had been a big mistake.

Maybe she's manic-depressive . . . he pondered . . . *or maybe she's coming down from being high on some sort of drug. Whatever it is, she's not emotionally stable. Maybe it's not a good idea to share a room with her tonight . . . she could be a sociopath . . .*

"Derek," she said, motioning for him to sit next to her on a bench, "there's something I need to tell you. You've been nice to me and . . . well . . . I like you and I don't want to lie to you about things . . ."

Her voice trailed off into silence. After a moment, she started talking again.

"You know . . . back at the end of the street where there was a bathroom?"

Derek nodded.

"Well, last night I slept in the trees just behind it."

"The truth is," she continued, "I don't have a place to sleep tonight, either. I'm sort of homeless at the moment, and I don't have any money left. I'm broke and I don't have anywhere to go, so . . ."

As she paused for a second time, Derek finished the sentence for her.

" . . . so you were wondering if you could spend the night in my motel room . . ."

This time it was Derek's turn to pause.

" . . . and you're hoping I'll take you out for dinner. Is that what you're trying to say?"

Vanessa dropped her eyes back to the ground and said, "Yeah, I guess that's close enough. So, is it all right? I mean, is it all right if I, you know, sleep in your room tonight? Just this one night? I'll leave after breakfast . . . they serve breakfast at the motel, don't they? Then I'll be gone. I promise I'll go. I just need help for tonight and then . . . I'll figure it out. It's not your problem. It's mine. So don't worry, it'll work out. It always does . . . most of the time . . . sometimes . . ."

She stopped talking and looked up at Derek's face, hoping to catch some sign of a positive response.

"Sure," he answered. "We can try it for one night, but on one condition."

"What's that?"

"I want you to promise you won't strangle me or cut my throat while I'm sleeping."

"What? That's a joke, right? You're joking—or do you mean you think that I'd . . ."

Vanessa stopped herself in mid-sentence and took a deep breath. Derek's words had taken her by surprise and she didn't know how to respond, or even whether she should respond at all. Was he testing her or teasing her? Maybe it *was* just a joke.

Maybe, she wondered, *just this once instead of getting mad . . .*

"Well, here's the thing," she said with a perfectly straight face, "Take your pick: I can either promise I won't kill you tonight, I can tell you to get lost and go to hell, or I can just strangle you now and get it over with."

It had been a long time since she had attempted to match wits with another person. When she was a child, her father—her real father—had constantly teased her with outlandish comments and then challenged her to reply in kind. It had been their special game and she loved him for it. When he died, however, the humor in the house had died with him.

178

Her verbal comeback to Derek reflected a playfulness she had not dared to indulge in since. Her attempt at repartee left her feeling vulnerable. She had trusted her father completely, but with Derek she wasn't so sure. There was something about him that reminded her of her father. Yet how, she wondered, could any man be as loving and kind as her father had been? She felt as if she had just jumped out of a window in a burning building not knowing if Derek was going to be there to catch her or not. She was in free-fall and the ground was about to . . .

"I'll take option number one," Derek replied. "Let's go get some dinner."

He reached over to touch her right hand but she pulled it away, stood up and raised it in the air.

"I, Vanessa," she declared, "do solemnly swear that I will not kill, murder or beat up Derek while he is asleep tonight. So help me God. Amen."

"That's good," he said smiling. "I was worried I was going to have to spend the night sitting in a corner of the room with a shotgun across my knees."

Vanessa begin to break into a smile, but she corralled it, sent it back where it came from and gave Derek an expressionless poke on the arm instead.

You got what you want, girl, she reminded herself. *Just take it and don't trust him with anything or you'll get burned again, for sure.*

The smile wasn't the only thing Vanessa was fighting against. She had found herself attracted to Derek in a way that frightened her. Since her father died, everything and everybody she had ever loved and cherished had been taken away from her. She did not want to go through that kind of pain and loss again; not with Derek, not with anyone.

"You remind me of a story," Derek offered as they reached the end of the Boardwalk and began retracing their morning walk past the kite festival vendors towards town. "It's about Jack Benny—he was a comedian and was on TV. Do you know who he is . . . or was?"

"Yeah, I guess," she answered.

"Well, I read how one time he went to Vermont to do a benefit show for a friend, but no matter how hard he tried, he couldn't get anybody in the theater to laugh. After the performance, he went up to his friend and said, 'I'm so sorry, that had to be the worst show I ever did. I totally bombed.' 'Oh, no,' the friend replied, 'you were wonderful. It took all we could do to keep from laughing.'"

Derek stopped walking and looked at Vanessa.

Vanessa stopped and looked at Derek.

"I don't get it," she said.

"You don't laugh or smile much either, do you," he said. "Why?"

She started to snap back with, "Because you're not funny," but checked herself.

She paused for a moment before answering with an honesty that surprised her.

"Because it hurts," she said.

Derek nodded as if he understood, then turned and started walking again with Vanessa quickly coming alongside.

"In that case," he said, as he flashed his usual smile, "I'll try not to say anything funny."

After a few more steps, he heard her say in a quiet, almost inaudible voice, "Ouch."

A quick glance showed him she was still not smiling.

Maybe the smile is inside, he thought. *Let's see if I can get it to come out and play.*

Sorry, Mom, he added as he wished his thoughts towards Willapa Bay and over the horizon beyond. *I know, I know: If she's broken I'll let God do the fixing, but until God shows up*

I'm just going to try and give a little push to get her started, okay?

"Look here," he said as they passed one of the t-shirt vendors, "I've never been a fan of Guns N' Roses so why don't you pick out a new shirt to wear for dinner."

Vanessa looked at the racks of t-shirts and then back at Derek unsure whether he was being serious or not.

"Go on," he said. "Do me a favor—anything but Guns N' Roses."

She spotted the one she wanted immediately. It was sky blue with a view of two kites flying side by side connected to two tiny people far below standing in what looked like a meadow.

"I'll take this one," she said. "There are two kites so they must be fighting with each other, right?"

Derek started to say they weren't the right kind of kites for fighting but changed his mind and simply said, "Good choice," instead.

"So . . . ?" Derek asked after paying for the shirt. "Where do you want to go for dinner?"

"Someplace with food," Vanessa answered flatly.

Some place nice, Derek thought to himself. *She might not get a chance to eat a decent meal again for a long time.*

"Let's eat here," he said at door of the first sit-down restaurant they came to. "They have a restroom where you can change."

After switching shirts, she rejoined Derek and ordered a seafood platter. By the time she finished eating there was nothing left on her plate but empty clamshells and scampi tails.

"Thanks for dinner," she said as they stood to leave, "and thanks for the shirt."

They spent the evening switching channels back and forth on the motel room television.

"My turn with the remote," Vanessa demanded, as Derek obediently tossed the device from where he was lying on his bed over to where she was lying on hers. She punched in a random number and brought up a History Channel documentary on Gutzon Borglum and Mt. Rushmore.

"Wait, don't change it," Derek shouted. "That's where I grew up! Rapid City, South Dakota. We used to drive over to Mt. Rushmore to have picnics. Did you know that there are trails that will take you all the way up . . . "

Vanessa clicked to a different station. At that moment, the last thing in the world she wanted to talk about was South Dakota.

Twelve more hours, she calculated, *and I'll be back on the street . . . unless I play my cards right . . ."*

"I'm tired," she abruptly announced. "You can watch what you want. I'm going to sleep."

Derek caught the remote just before it nailed him on the forehead.

"No," he said as he switched off the television. "I'm tired, too. I hope you sleep well. After what you told me about last night . . ."

He couldn't think how to finish the sentence so he simply dropped the thought and headed for the bathroom.

He was surprised at how nervous he suddenly felt about sharing the room with Vanessa. Although he had spent most of the day with her, he still knew little or nothing about her except that she had promised not to murder him during the night. Normally he would have only worn sleep shorts to bed, but as he changed out of his clothes, he added a t-shirt hoping it might make things less awkward than they already were. When he emerged from the bathroom, he saw that Vanessa was already tucked under her blanket with her eyes closed.

So much for modesty, he decided.

As he turned off his bedside light, he noticed Vanessa had draped her pants, t-shirt and bra over a chair. He left it for his imagination to decide what she was wearing under the blankets.

For a few minutes, he lay awake, listening to Vanessa's slow, soft, rhythmic breathing. Then he yawned, rolled over with his back to her, and fell asleep.

Thirty minutes later Vanessa slipped out of her bed and climbed into Derek's. As she noiselessly slid her hand under his shirt and began gently rubbing his back, she felt herself embraced by his warmth.

This is nice, she thought to herself.

In the safety of darkness, she allowed herself the luxury of breaking into a contented smile. With other men, she had assumed an unspoken obligation to meet whatever physical or emotional need they might have had at any given moment. Tonight, however, with Derek it was different. He had not indicated he wanted anything from her at all—except friendship. As she idly ran her index finger along his spine, she found herself torn between the old sense of obligation and a new feeling of freedom—the freedom to touch him and love him not because he expected it of her, but because she desired it for herself.

She removed her hand from under his shirt and stretched it out across his hip and down.

The touch of her hand on his hip woke him. In one quick movement, he grasped her hand, pushed it back and rolled over so that he was lying face to face with her.

"You don't have to do this," he said quietly.

"I know," she whispered.

His hand brushed along her body and encountered nothing but skin. He found himself filled with a desire to touch more of her but, with great effort, he let go of her hand and pulled his own away.

"It's just . . . " he said, searching for words, " . . . it's just that I don't know if it's a good idea . . . I mean . . . to get carried away like this tonight."

He paused to give her time to respond.

"Why?" she asked. "Are you gay?"

He smiled in the darkness.

"No," he said, "It's because we just met and . . . well . . . making love means something to me that . . . well . . . people should take more time before . . ."

He couldn't find the words to express what he was feeling.

"So?" she asked. "I should go back to my bed?"

"No," he said hesitantly. "I mean, if you want to lie next to me that would be all right, I guess. But I'll face the other way. We can keep warm together."

"I want to be close to you . . . as close as you'll let me," she said

"I'd like that, too," he said, not sure whether it was his heart or his flesh that had spoken the words. "But for tonight we can just be friends, okay?"

Vanessa buried her face between his shoulder blades and answered with a muffled, "Uh, huh."

Within moments, they were breathing in unison, their lives separated by nothing more than the thin cotton fabric of Derek's shirt.

"I had a girl . . ."

He spoke the words into the darkness so softly he could hardly hear them himself.

"She said she loved me and I said the same."

He waited for a response, but all he heard was Vanessa's breathing and the sound of his own heart beating.

"We were both eighteen," he continued. "I gave her a ring and she said, 'Yes.'"

There was still no response.

"After I enlisted and went to boot camp she dropped off the face of the earth. I never saw or heard from her again. When I came home, she was gone. Even her parents didn't know where she was. They found my ring sitting on her dresser. There wasn't even a note . . ."

His voice drifted into silence with the words, "Eight years . . . and I'm still waiting . . ."

Derek fell asleep with the warmth of Vanessa's breath on the back of his neck. He assumed she had fallen asleep long before, but he was wrong. She had heard every word.

*   *   *   *

"What am I supposed to do, now?"

The words were accompanied by a burst of light.

Derek sat up in bed, shielding his blinking eyes from the sunshine streaming through the motel room window. In the midst of the glare, he could see the silhouette of a fully clothed female.

"Vanessa, what time is it?"

"It's seven o'clock and, as you can see, it's morning."

"Are you . . ."

Vanessa cut him off in mid-thought.

"What am I supposed to do, now?" she shouted for the second time.

"What are you supposed to do about *what*?" he questioned back.

"I mean, you let me spend the night—that was nice. And you bought me dinner, right? But now it's today and I'm supposed to just say, 'Good-bye,' and walk out the door, is that it? Well it's all crap, you pretending to be nice and everything. It's all crap. I guess it's time for me to go to hell and you can go fly a kite . . ."

"Is that the best you can do?" Derek interrupted with a laugh. "I mean, you know more swear words than a pirate and the best you can come up with is to tell me to 'go fly a kite?'"

185

She charged him with fists clenched and arms flailing.

"It's not funny," she screamed, as she swung her fists at his face. "I'm sick and tired of your stupid smile. I busted your lip yesterday but this time . . ."

Derek fended off the blows, grabbed her around the waist, pulled her onto the bed and held her tightly to himself. He did this partly in self-defense but also in the hope that holding her might give her time to calm down.

"Let me go," she screamed. "I hate you, I hate you, I hate you . . ."

There was a knock on the door and Derek could see the outline of someone staring at them through the window.

"It's okay," Derek shouted back. "She's upset about something and . . ."

"I need to hear that from her, not you," came a voice, "or else I'll call the police."

Vanessa went limp in Derek's arms.

"No police," she whispered frantically. "No police! Tell him 'No police!'"

"You tell him," Derek said as he swung her onto the side of the bed and stood her on her feet. "He wants to hear it from you."

She had started crying again, just as she had the day before. For a moment, she stood staring at the door, but then, without a word, she turned back to Derek and fell onto the bed, sobbing.

"Just a second," Derek called, as he crawled over her heaving body.

He walked over to the door and opened it.

"You're the manager, right?" he asked.

"No," said the man, "I'm the guy in the room next door. What's going on?"

Derek stepped away from the door, pointed towards the bed and said, "There she is. Ask her yourself."

"Ma'am," he said, "are you all right?"

Vanessa sat up on the edge of the bed and managed to sniffle out the words, "Don't call me 'Ma'am,' okay? Please don't . . . I mean I'm . . . It's fine. I'm fine. Derek is fine. Everything's fine. I'm just upset . . . like he said . . . I just need a minute to calm down. He didn't hurt me or anything, if that's what you're thinking.

"See?" she said as she stood up, walked across the room and stood face to face with the man at the door. "Look at me. I'm fine. Really. I'm fine. So . . . just go back to your room and I'll be quiet and . . . and it'll be fine, okay? Thanks. Maybe we'll see you at breakfast."

She gently closed the door and then did the same with the curtains.

As she slumped into a chair, Derek knelt next to her.

"You don't hate me," he said. "I think it's something else. Am I right?"

Vanessa nodded.

"You want to stay with me because you don't have anywhere else to go, right?"

Vanessa started to nod, "Yes," but stopped herself and looked up.

"No," she said, "that's not it."

She stood up and walked across the room with her back to Derek.

"I mean, 'Yes,' that's part of it but I'm okay with that. It's just that . . ."

She paused, turned around and continued in an intense whisper, "I like you . . . I love you . . . I think . . . I mean . . . I don't know what I mean . . . it's just that you're different and I don't want to . . . to lose you . . ."

As Vanessa talked, Derek stood up, walked to where she was standing and wrapped his arms around her. For the first time since they met, she did not pull away from his touch.

"I like you, too," he said quietly. "I'm not sure about the 'love' part of it, though. If it's okay with you, we can just be friends and see what happens. I'm here in town for another two days, so you can stay with me and . . . well . . . I'd like it if you'd . . . you know . . . for two days . . . we can talk about it and figure it out."

Vanessa put her hands on Derek's shoulders, gently pushed him away and looked at him with sad eyes, still wet from tears.

"Okay," she said softly. "Thank you for being so kind. I don't deserve it . . . no one has ever been this nice to me before."

"I don't think you hate my smile, either," he said, smiling. "At least I hope you don't, because I do it all the time. It's like a bad habit."

For a fleeting moment, Derek thought he saw a hint of a smile appear and then disappear from Vanessa's face.

"I like your smile," she said without offering one of her own. "You can keep it."

Derek's smile grew a little bigger as he added, "If you want me to eat breakfast with you you're going to have to let me change into something more appropriate than sleep shorts."

There was plenty to eat for breakfast and Derek was impressed with how much of it Vanessa was able to consume.

"Well," she said between bites, "did you marry her?"

"Marry who?"

"The girl you were talking about last night. You said you gave her a ring and you said she was gone when you came back from boot camp, but you didn't say whether or not you married her in between."

Derek put his plastic fork on the table and paused to consider why she was asking the question and how he should answer it.

188

"I know it's none of my business," Vanessa continued, "but I was just curious since, at the end, you said you were still waiting."

"I thought you were asleep when I said that," Derek answered. "But, if you really want to know, we never got married, and when I said I was still waiting . . . well, I didn't mean I was still waiting for her to come back, I meant . . . that I'm still waiting for the right girl . . ."

He stopped in mid sentence and looked at Vanessa as if he was seeing her for the first time. He saw that she was beautiful—but he had already seen that. He also saw she was damaged goods and that even God might not be able to fix the parts of her that seemed to be broken—but this, too, he had already seen in her. What he saw this time, and what he had not seen before, was a young woman who had just a few minutes earlier said she was in love with him. Was it possible, he wondered, for him to fall in love with her? As the thought raced through his mind, he heard himself finish his answer to Vanessa.

" . . . waiting for the right girl to come along and . . . well, it hasn't happened . . . yet . . . not yet."

Vanessa searched his eyes for a moment before returning her attention to her Belgian waffle.

When she was finished eating, Derek asked if she'd like to learn how to fly a kite.

"I know you're not into kites, but give it a try, you might like it. Until I tried it in Afghanistan I had no idea how much fun it could be."

Vanessa nodded, "Why not, I've got nothing else to do."

In the back of Derek's car a collection of carry-bags were stacked like cordwood.

"Here's a small Delta," he explained as he pulled one out and handed it to Vanessa. "It's fun to fly because it's got two strings so it can be turned and steered in different directions. You carry it. I'll assemble it when we get to the beach."

He reached in and took a second bag from the top of the pile.

"This is the one I was flying yesterday," he said as he locked the trunk and started walking towards the beach. "It's a Japanese kite called a Rokkaku—the kind used in kite fighting."

It was another warm, cloudless day with a gentle wind perfect for kites.

That morning the featured displays at the festival were kite strings. Already four people had let out long nylon cords with a colorful triangular kite attached every six feet or so. If Vanessa had bothered to count them, she would found two strings with sixty or seventy kites on each string, one with eighty and one with over a hundred. The uppermost kites were so far up in the sky they seemingly vanished into nothingness.

Vanessa's interest in kites, however, did not go any further than her interest in Derek. As he unpacked the kites and assembled them on the beach Vanessa watched as his hands and arms shimmered in the morning sunlight. She watched as his fingers moved the way a musician's fingers move when they are playing an instrument. She watched as his face and eyes danced back and forth between his various tasks, and she watched as the toes on his bare feet unconsciously dug holes in the sand.

"Here," he said when he had finished, "let's start with the Delta."

"No," Vanessa said, curtly, "I want to fly the other one, the one you fight with."

They were the first words she had spoken since they had left the breakfast room at the motel.

Without questioning her choice, Derek secured the Delta to the ground and picked up the Rok. It was a six-sided kite that stood nearly as tall as Vanessa. On the front surface of the kite was the face of a scowling Samurai warrior, painted in a Japanese style.

Although it was the same kite that had landed next to her the previous morning and the same kite she had been watching Derek assemble, she had never bothered to look at the kite itself until that moment.

"It's beautiful," she said loudly enough for Derek to hear. "Aren't you afraid you'll break it?"

"Kites are like people," he answered. "They are fragile, they are wonderfully made, and they are capable of doing amazing things. But you're right, they can be damaged. That's the risk we take when we let them fly . . . just like people. We can live our lives playing it safe, sitting around like couch potatoes, growing old and fat but that's not why God made us. God made us to fly, and if we fly, we're going to get banged up from time to time . . ."

". . . and," Vanessa added, "there will people trying to cut us down, like in kite fighting, right?"

"Yes," Derek nodded, "there's always that."

The breeze rattled the kite and the conversation entered a short period of silence until Derek moved it forward again with words.

"Vanessa?" he asked. "Do you want to fly? I mean, are you ready to see if you can soar like a kite and see life in a new way? I think you've been held down on the ground for too long. You're beautiful, you're smart, and you're funny, too, but you're keeping it all stuffed inside."

Vanessa felt the old anger rising again. She clenched her fists and fought the urge to charge at him again.

I am not *beautiful!* She screamed silently to herself. *I am* not *smart!*

She put her hands over her ears and began swaying back and forth.

Shut up, Derek! Go to hell and leave me alone! I'm ugly and stupid . . .

She turned to run away, but when she felt Derek's hand touch her shoulder she froze in place, unsure whether she was weak enough to leave or strong enough to stay.

"Here . . ."

The voice was a man's voice—a voice she had heard for the first time in this same spot the previous morning. It was a voice that had startled her, frightened her and angered her. Yet it was a kind voice—a gentle voice—a loving voice. It was Derek's voice.

"Here . . . take it," said the voice. "Make it fly!"

As she turned back and faced Derek, he placed the kite string reel in her hands and lifted the kite into the air.

"Let the string run free!" He shouted, looking like a small boy who had just peeked under the living room tree on Christmas morning.

"I don't know how!" Vanessa shouted back, terrified that something bad was going to happen.

"Here . . .," said the voice, "I'll show you."

Derek turned and stood next to her. With her hands held in his he showed how to release the string, how to control how fast it ran out, and how to lock it in place.

In a matter of seconds, the kite swept high into the sky, with the Samurai warrior staring down at them as if Vanessa and Derek had become the two small figures on her t-shirt.

Tears welled up in her eyes and the smile she had kept locked up in the darkest corner of her soul broke free.

"Damn you, Derek!" she shouted. "Go to hell and leave me alone!"

Derek stepped back and stared at her, totally confused by the sudden outburst.

192

What he saw was a beautiful young woman flying the most precious kite he owned while wearing the most beautiful smile he had ever seen.

"Well?" she asked cryptically as if she was Jack Benny and Derek was the audience in a New England theater.

The moment hit him over the head with the subtlety of a sledgehammer. He began laughing so hard he had to sit down on the sand to catch his breath.

"Okay," he said, after inhaling and exhaling slowly a few times, "here it comes."

After allowing for a short, dramatic pause, he shouted in a voice loud enough to be heard above the festival loudspeaker system, "What you need is a new scriptwriter!"

The wind caught their laughter and carried it high above the beach and across the Peninsula to the farthest corners of the earth. The heavens joined in the laughter and even the Samurai warrior did his best to send a smile down on the two small figures far below.

All stories end, of course, and this story is no exception. The only thing unusual about the way this particular story ends is that it ends with a poem.

On the Wings of the Wind

Come with me take my hand,
We will walk we will run,
We will reach for the stars if we dare.
We will rise, we will stand,
We will dance with the sun,
With the whisper of wind in our hair.

Like two kites in the sky
On the wings of the wind,
We will fly on the wings of the wind.
We will fly hand in hand,
We will dream, we will love,
As we dance on the wings of the wind.

Let me take you away,
Leave the past in the past,
Let the wind fill your sails and be free.
There is night there is day,
Choose the light; hold it fast;
Touch the clouds, breathe the air, come with me.

Like two kites in the sky
On the wings of the wind,
We will fly on the wings of the wind
We will fly hand in hand,
We will dream, we will love,
As we dance on the wings of the wind.

Years have passed, and the cord
That has tied us to earth
Has grown thin and will soon break away.
We have flown, we have soared,
We have lived out our birth,
But we'll soar even higher that day!

Like two kites in the sky
On the wings of the wind,
We will fly on the wings of the wind.
We will fly hand in hand,
We will dream, we will love,
As we dance on the wings of the wind.
Come with me on the wings of the wind.

Full Circle

"We are here today to give thanks to God as we remember and celebrate Carter Latti's good life . . ."

As he spoke, Pastor Ron Patterson was pleased to note that the church was full to overflowing. There were only a few empty places left in the pews and even the seats along the side wall where the choir usually sat had been taken. There were a half-dozen men standing against the back wall, and through the open entry doors, he could see Don Milner from the funeral chapel helping the ushers set up folding chairs in the narthex to accommodate the latecomers.

Too bad it's not this full on Sundays, he thought.

As his lips continued reading the opening words of the funeral liturgy his mind took a detour to consider why people who would ordinarily show no interest in Jesus or the church would take the time and make the effort to show up for a funeral service. It was a simple question, but before he could begin to sift through the possible answers, his thoughts began to merge back onto the main road.

"I am the Resurrection and the Life," Ron read, quoting Jesus' words from the Gospel of John. "Those who believe in me, even though they die, will live, and everyone who lives and believes in me will never die . . .'"

Unlike most of the folks who had come to pay him their respects, Carter was a man who had taken both Jesus and the church seriously. Over the years, he had served as an elder, deacon, Sunday school teacher, and youth leader. When it came to the church, there wasn't much that Carter and his wife, Marian, hadn't been involved with at one time or another. He had been active in the community as well. As the owner of one of Long Beach's largest tourist shops, he had served on both the city council and the chamber of commerce. He was born and raised on the Peninsula and was a close friend or a distant relation to just about everybody this side of the Lower Columbia. Because of these relationships, his death, on this particular day at least, had gotten more people to come to church than Jesus' death and resurrection combined.

Carter's friends and fellow church members Bob and Jean were sitting in their usual pew, stage left towards the back. They were not used to sitting so close to so many people.

"Good turnout for Carter," Bob whispered, as he leaned over to get as close to Jean's ear as possible.

"Shhh, he's talking," Jean replied with a whisper of her own and a slight head nod towards the front of the church.

"Do you think there will be enough cookies at the reception?" Bob whispered back.

This time Jean replied by gently, but firmly, fastening her fingernails into his upper leg.

Bob decided he would wait until after the service to find out about the cookies.

"Let us pray," Pastor Ron continued. "Almighty God, in whom we live and move and have our being . . ."

Bel McCrae slipped silently into the space her husband, Cole, had saved for her in their usual pew, halfway back, stage right.

"Is everything good in the kitchen?" Cole whispered.

"Yes, but I can't believe how bad it smells," Bel answered.

Cole, who was hard of hearing, wondered who had gotten mad in the kitchen, but he didn't want to disrupt the service with another question so he let it go until later.

" . . . who can take the darkness of our grief and turn it into the brilliant light of the morning . . ."

Pete and Colin and their wives were sitting towards the front on Pastor Ron's left while Marty, Pete's former fisherman friend and betrayer sat in the choir area surrounded by people he recognized but didn't remember by name. Since the choir chairs were at right angles to the pews, Marty had Pete directly in his line of sight. At first, he tried to avoid looking at him but as the service moved along his eyes became fixed on the face of the man whose life he had intentionally and maliciously tried to ruin. Over the years, his heart, in the biblical sense of the word, had become hardened against his old friend. Now, as he recalled memories of the good times he and Pete had shared before their falling out, he felt the last of that hardness begin to slip away.

" . . . and forgive us our sins as we forgive those who sin against us . . ."

As Pete spoke the words of the Lord's Prayer in unison with the rest of the congregation, he turned his head to look at Marty. For a moment, and for the first time in years, their eyes met.

Marty's eyes said, "I'm sorry."

Pete's eyes said, "I forgive you."

Although they didn't discover it until later, at that moment they had become friends once again.

" . . . Carter's grandfather, Pavo Lahti, and Pavo's brother came to Ilwaco from Finland back in 1901. In 1919, Pavo returned to Finland with his wife and a three-year old son named August who would one day become Carter's father. In 1936, at the age of 20, August returned to Ilwaco and discovered the Immigration Service had changed the spelling of his name from 'Lahti,' to 'Latti.' He didn't argue the point so that explains why there are both Lahtis and Lattis on the Peninsula and why they are all part of the same family . . ."

As a favor to the family, Pastor Ron was reading a statement about Carter's life written by Carter's son, who had been unable to attend. Although Ron had been serving the church as pastor for two years, he figured most of the people in front of him had known Carter far better than he had. Because of this, he was happy to have a member of Carter's family share a memory and a story or two during the service, even if he was the one who wound up reading it.

As he came to the end of the written text, he felt moved to add a few personal words of his own.

"One of the best things about being a pastor is the opportunity it provides to meet and get to know some of the most interesting people in the world. For me, Carter was one of those people . . ."

Ron noticed a few of the women and many of the men nodding their heads in agreement, including Punk Suomi who was sitting with his Ilwaco neighbor Potsy. Punk, who had known Carter since the day he was born, had lost his own wife to cancer some years earlier. It didn't seem fair to him that he was now outliving friends who were younger than himself.

Encouraged by the positive response to his last comment, Pastor Ron decided to add a few more words before turning the microphone over to Carter's daughter, Elise.

"One of the things Carter enjoyed more than anything else was clamming . . ."

One or two heads nodded in agreement but, at the reference to clams, the rest of the gathered assemblage became strangely still, as if everyone in the room had decided to hold their breath at the same time.

"It was one of the things that he and Marian enjoyed doing together and, after her death, he continued to dig for clams as often as possible . . ."

The sound of several men clearing their throats broke the silence.

"In fact," Ron continued, "I don't think I've ever known anyone who loved clams as much as Carter . . ."

The throat clearing increased to near epidemic proportions, accompanied by a rising crescendo of whispers punctuated by what sounded like someone desperately attempting to suppress a laugh.

Ron could tell he had said something wrong but he had no idea what it was. As an experienced speaker, he knew he had three choices. He could let the moment pass and keep on with what he was saying; He could take a step back and try to salvage his mistake, or; He could simply stop talking and give the mike to Elise.

He made his decision without missing a beat.

"Clams or no clams," he continued, "what Carter loved more than anything else was his family. His daughter, Elise, would now like to share a few words about her father."

"Thank you, Pastor Patterson, and thank you for spending so much time with Dad during the last few weeks. Dad was a good man, a good husband, and a good father. He loved everyone, and I know he considered each of you here today to be a dear friend. He was that sort of a man. He loved life and everything that life had to offer. He considered himself lucky to have spent his life here on the Peninsula and boasted to everyone he met about what an amazing place it is.

"Even during the last months of his life he never let the cancer get the best of him. If we asked him how he was doing he'd just smile and say, 'I'm not dead yet!'

"Those of you who knew my mom know how much she loved clams and those of you who knew my dad know how much he enjoyed digging for them. What some of you may not know is that my mother hated digging for clams and my father must have been one of the only people on the Peninsula who didn't like eating them. This made them a perfect team. Mom would go with Dad to dig clams, Dad would bring them home and clean them, and then Mom would cook them and eat them while Dad ate something else. "

Pastor Ron felt the sudden urge to lean over to the person sitting next to him and whisper the words, "I didn't know that." But since he was sitting by himself at the front of the church he had to keep his thoughts to himself. Others in the church, he noticed, were doing the whispering for him.

One of the whisperers was Thelma Mulroney. Thelma wasn't a member of the church but she had come to the service because she had been a close friend of Carter's wife. She knew that Carter wasn't particularly fond of clams so when Elise asked her to make clam fritters for his funeral reception she couldn't understand why.

"They'll be cold and soggy by the time people get around to eating them," she told Elise.

"Don't worry about it," Elise replied as she handed Thelma a quart sized freezer bag filled with frozen razor clams."

Ruth Marshall, whose interests rotated between baking cookies and scanning the Peninsula with her metal detector, was sitting with her husband, Benny and wondering the same thing. Several days earlier, Elise had given her a hand-written recipe along with instructions to, "Just do it and don't ask me why, okay?"

She had done what Elise asked her to do but had not worked up the courage to taste any of the cookies she had baked. Even Norm, her close friend and neighbor who loved cookies more than anything else in the world had to be coerced into taking just one bite. He chewed for a while before putting the cookie back on the plate.

"I can't wait to see how this turns out at the reception," he said without a trace of his usual smile.

Today, Norm was sitting in the choir section, listening to Elise's words with the look of someone waiting to hear the punch line to a joke.

"When Mom died," Elise continued, "Dad kept digging the clams, cleaning the clams and freezing the clams but he didn't eat them or give any of them away. My guess is that it became a sort of compulsive/obsessive way for him to deal with losing Mom. For a long time, Dad has kept the garage locked up when any of us came for a visit. We figured it was because the garage was messy or unsafe for the grandchildren. It turns out that when Dad ran out of space for the frozen clams in the kitchen refrigerator he bought a freezer and put it in the garage. When that filled up, he bought another freezer. When he died two weeks ago, we found four freezers in the garage filled with somewhere close to 3,500 razor clams. It seems that Dad has been driving to Oregon to dig clams when he couldn't dig them here at the Beach."

With the punch line in sight, Norm's wry, whimsical smile was rapidly expanding into a broad grin.

"Even though most of us in the family love clams as much as Mom we couldn't agree on what to do with them. There were too many for us to use ourselves and we didn't want to waste them by throwing them away. So, we decided we'd get rid of the things by using them for Dad's funeral reception and by giving them away to those of you who do enjoy razor clams. Finally, as a sort of farewell joke on Dad, we've tried to prepare them every way we could imagine.

"So . . . please eat as much as you can at the reception. Feel free to take as many leftovers as you can carry, and please . . . *please* take home as many bags of Dad's goddamn clams as you can fit in your car!"

"*Bon Apetit!*"

Elise nodded at Pastor Ron and sat down with her family in the front pew.

The whispering in the room stopped cold while everyone stared at Ron to see what he was going to say or do next.

Across the aisle and three pews back from the McCraes sat the Tuppencethalers. The family was in church because Mr. Tuppencethaler had been Carter's friend and the manager of his store. The three Tuppencethaler children had been completely bored by the service until Elise spoke the word colloquially synonymous with the phrase, "divine judgment to hell."

Five-year old Tara looked up at her sixteen-year old brother and whispered, "Steve? Did she just say, 'goddamn?' Isn't that a bad word?"

Seven-year old Tommy started giggling and Mrs. Tuppencethaler couldn't decide whether to put her hands over Tara's ears or start laughing herself.

Pastor Ron had planned to read a passage from the Bible immediately after Elise finished sharing her thoughts about her father. But her closing use of a word not usually found in traditional Christian liturgical texts forced him to rethink the wisdom of moving straight from "goddamn" to "Thus saith the Lord" without stretching out the space between them just a little.

"Why don't we take a moment to silently and prayerfully thank God for how Carter's life has touched our own."

He nodded a cue to the organist who quietly began playing through one verse of "It Is Well with My Soul." When the music stopped, Ron was ready to begin talking again.

"During his ministry Jesus spoke of many things but, so far as I know, he never expressed an opinion on the subject of clams."

Ron's attempt at humor and the laughter that followed managed to break the tension created by Elise's colorful vocabulary-malfunction. As the laughter subsided, Ron began to share some words he had both carefully and lovingly prepared for the occasion.

"Some of the things Jesus *did* talk about were life, death, and resurrection.

"'I am the resurrection and the life,' he said. 'The one who believes in me will live, even though they die.'

"Elise told us how Carter adopted the phrase, 'I'm not dead yet,' as his end of life motto. I think Jesus would have approved of it, not only as a motto for Carter, but as a motto for each of us here today . . . "

Ron's words may have been "carefully prepared" but no one paid much attention to them. Nor, for that matter, did anyone pay much attention to anything else during the rest of the service. People's eyes began to glaze over as visions of razor clams danced in their heads. The only head-nodding Pastor Ron saw during his closing words was when someone looked down to check the time on his or her watch. Folks had come to pay their respects to Carter but now they were ready to leave, go to the reception, and check out all the "goddamn clams."

". . . and we commit Carter Latti's soul to the care and mercy of Almighty God, in the sure and certain hope of resurrection to eternal life."

The four friends, Phil, Shannon, Benny, Roger and their wives were sitting in one of the back pews. This, they thought, would make it easier for them to get in and out of the church with Phil's cane and Shannon's walker. To avoid the anticipated rush they were half-way out the back door before Pastor Ron came to the end of his closing benediction. At the sound of the word, "Amen," the stampede to the reception began. Carter's family and Pastor Ron found themselves stranded at the front of the sanctuary where they formed the tail end of a line that pushed and shoved its way impatiently into the fellowship hall.

What people discovered when they entered the reception was the aroma of fried, baked, steamed, smoked, grilled, chopped, diced and sliced razor clams. There were three kinds of clam chowder and two kinds of clam dip. There were clam fritters and clam cakes, clams fried with garlic and clams fried with jalapeño peppers. There were clam kabobs, clam paté, clam sausage and clam casserole. There was clam juice, clamato juice and, oddly enough, cranclam juice alongside clam infused coffee and tea. Lastly, on the dessert table were clam cookies, clam brownies and a frosted sheet cake with clams in it.

Bel McCrae stood nearby describing how Elise had given her a large bag of frozen clams along with instructions to bake her famous cranberry brownies with clams instead of cranberries.

"Just do it," Elise said.

Bel didn't say it out loud, but the brownies turned out to be the worst thing she had ever made. They smelled bad, they tasted awful and even her dog, who would ordinarily eat anything, turned up his nose and walked away when she offered him one.

As far as planning the reception was concerned, it wasn't clear whether Elise had been as crazy as a fox or had simply lost her mind entirely. What was clear to everyone, however, was that the reception was a huge success.

By the time Pastor Ron managed to squeeze his way into the fellowship hall the soup, the dip, the casserole and just about everything else that looked palatable had been eaten. The dessert table, however, appeared to have been hardly touched.

The first person Ron met was Tommy Tuppencethaler who held something up to his face.

"Here, Pastor Ron. It's a chocolate covered clam. They're great. I'll get you one if you want . . ."

"No thank you, Tommy. I'll try one later, maybe, okay?"

"Okay, Pastor. This is the best party ever!"

And off he went.

Eventually the conversations ran their course and the crowd thinned as people carried bags of frozen razor clams to their cars and rushed home to get them into their freezers before they started to thaw

Soon the cleanup began as the women took charge of the kitchen and the men put away the tables and chairs.

Because of their physical limitations, Phil and Shannon sat and chatted with Pastor Ron and Don Milner who had helped set the whole thing up.

"Nice service," Shannon said.

"It was a good sendoff for Carter," Phil added.

"That it was," Ron replied as he absentmindedly reached across the table, picked up a brownie and popped it into his mouth.

"Are you sure that was a good idea?" Shannon asked.

Ron's stomach immediately knew the correct answer was, "No."

"I'll be right back," Ron whispered as he stood up, doubled over, and headed as fast as he could to the men's room across the hall.

Five minutes later, he staggered back and sat down, looking pale with just a hint of green around the edges.

"Feeling better, Pastor?" Shannon asked.

"I'm not dead yet."

"If you change your mind," added Don, "give me a call."

"You never know," said Phil.

The four men laughed.

And somewhere nearby, just beyond their sight, Carter laughed with them.

Also by James A. Tweedie

Mike Maurison—Private Eye
4-Novel Series

I Want My MoMA (Book 1)
A Year in the Life of Mike Maurison, Private Eye

To Have and To Hold (Book 2)
A Month in the Life of Mike Maurison, Private Eye

Treasure Hunt (Book 3)
A Week in the Life of Mike Maurison, Private Eye

Smoke and Mirrors (Book 4)
A Day in the Life of Mike Maurison, Private Eye

Long Beach Short Stories
Possibly Untrue Tales from the Pacific Northwest

Cycles
Coming of Age in an Ancient Time on a Distant World

The One Who Tells the Stories
A Boy, a Girl, One Week, and God

All books are available for purchase in paperback or Kindle at
Amazon.com

Made in the USA
Middletown, DE
08 August 2020